OPERATION BAMBOO GARDEN

OPERATION BAMBOO GARDEN

ANURAG ANAND

Vitasta

Published by
Renu Kaul Verma
Vitasta Publishing Pvt Ltd
4348/4C, Ansari Road, Daryaganj
New Delhi-110 002
info@vitastapublishing.com

ISBN: 978-81-19670-30-7

First Edition 2024
MRP ₹395

Edited by Abhijit Baroi
Typeset & Cover Design by Somesh Kumar Mishra
Printed by Vikas Computer and Printers, New Delhi

War is the spectacular and bloody projection of our everyday life. It is an outward expression of our inward state, an enlargement of our daily action.

—J Krishnamurti

CHAPTER 1

The Mighty Take A Tumble

Mumbai, 4th August 2020

The black Mercedes was racing down the Eastern Express Highway, honking and swerving past the few other vehicles on the road.

The state of Maharashtra had been at the eye of the Covid-19 pandemic, and Mumbai, the city of dreams, was yet to wake up from one of its worst-ever nightmares. The Corona case count in the Maximum City had breached the one hundred-thousand mark, even as the death toll remained mounting with each passing day. Fresh restrictions on travel and movement were being imposed at a disturbing regularity—perhaps a manifestation of the authorities' frustrations in clipping the wings of the deadly virus—leaving the common folk in a state of utter ambiguity and confusion.

The supposedly simple process of applying for and obtaining permissions for vehicular movement was proving to be very difficult. From a portal that wasn't designed to withstand the barrage of applications that were pouring in, to the inconsistent yardsticks being used by authorities to grant such approvals, the process was proving to be a game of chance for most.

The black Mercedes had a sticker affixed to its windshield proclaiming that the vehicle was approved for *Emergency Movement* across the state. It was therefore among the handful of private vehicles in the city that were not bound by lockdown related restrictions. This, and the sheer abandon with which the car zipped towards its destination, spoke of its occupant being a man of certain means and influence.

'Towards Vashi, Sir?' the driver, Mohsin, enquired. Mohsin had been in Ramanathan's employ for nine years and he couldn't recall a single instance when his employer had kept their destination concealed from him well into the drive. Ramanathan was a methodical man and he liked to make his hours on the road count. Invariably he would tell Mohsin where they were headed while boarding the vehicle and remain glued to his phone or laptop for remainder of the journey. He trusted Mohsin's instincts and his sense of traffic.

Today was different though.

'Take the Eastern Express highway,' was all that Ramanathan said as Mohsin shut the car door behind him. His grave and solemn look had prevented the driver from querying further. Ramanathan wasn't carrying his laptop or even his usual office bag. His phone was obviously with him, but Mohsin didn't see him draw it out. Instead, Ramanathan kept looking out the window, his eyes affixed on something obscure in the distance.

'Sir, should I take the turn towards Vashi?' after a brief wait Mohsin enquired again. A decision needed to be made. If they continued straight, they would exit Mumbai and enter the Thane district. And, if their destination happened to be Vashi, Mohsin would have to take the next exit and turn right towards the Vashi bridge.

'Uh... oh yes,' Ramanathan responded, emerging from his reverie. 'Take the turn towards the bridge.'

'And once you cross the toll booth, please stop on the side for a few minutes,' he added as an afterthought. Mohsin nodded, turned on the indicator and shifted his focus on changing lanes.

'Shall we stop here, Sir?' Mohsin asked. Given the sparse traffic, it took them all of five minutes to take the turn and cross the unmanned toll plaza. They were now on the Vashi bridge—one of the four entry points to the satellite city of Mumbai, built over the Thane creek.

'Yes, this is fine... Just wait inside the car,' Ramanathan said, stepping out of the vehicle. On a normal day, the bumper-to-bumper traffic on the bridge would have made such a halt impossible. But the pandemic had blurred the lines between the normal and the unusual in multiple respects.

Ramanathan walked away from the car and extracted his mobile phone from the jacket pocket. He looked towards the azure sky and heaved a deep sigh. It was a beautiful day and the slight breeze, as it brushed past his face, felt good. He looked over his shoulder, perhaps to check if he was adequately distanced from the vehicle, before bringing the phone screen to life.

'Suppu, can you imagine that it's been twenty years since we first met? I still remember our first coffee date... it was as though the cat had got my tongue. I was so nervous that I couldn't put a single coherent sentence together. I feared that I had messed it all up, but you obviously saw something in me and decided to give me another chance... And what a journey it has been ever since,' Ramanathan started dictating the voice message, pillaging through his memories and looking for the right words to express himself.

'Over the coming days and weeks, you will hear a lot of things... bad and ugly things and I hope you find it within you to stand by again then. You know that your happiness means the world to me and that is all I have ever cared about. And today, if I am doing something that will bring you nothing but pain and misery, it is because I am left with no alternatives... Please forgive me, my love. I love you, Suppu,' he said, releasing the microphone icon that would send the message to its intended recipient.

Putting the phone back inside the pocket, he looked at the skies and sighed once again. Then, in a flash, he grabbed the bridge's railing with one hand and flung himself across.

Mohsin, who had been watching his employer's actions from the confines of the car, was too stunned to react instantly. It was as if a gargantuan mallet had come crashing down on him out of nowhere. It took him a few seconds to process the scene his eyes were relaying back to his brain.

When he was able to regain control of his senses, he rushed out of the car screaming. Flailing his hands wildly, he ran towards the spot where he had last seen his employer standing. But by the time he craned his neck and peered down, all he could see were the concentric ripples in the otherwise placid waters of Thane creek.

CHAPTER 2

Decisions And Destiny

New Delhi, 4th August 2020

'Boss, have you reached home yet?'

'Just about to reach,' Ronit replied, one hand resting on the steering wheel, and his eyes peeled in search of a vacant parking spot.

The Type-4 Government Quarters in RK Puram had been allocated to officials from departments ranging from Animal Husbandry to Education over the years, making the area a true petri dish of human diversity. Many of these residents were working from home on account of the pandemic, and their vehicles, like obstinate tenants, rarely vacated the slots they were parked in.

Unfortunately, Ronit was bereft of any such privileges. Every morning, while steering the Hyundai hatchback out of its place, he would mouth a silent prayer seeking divine intervention to find an agreeable spot for the car upon his return from work. Given the limited number of slots in circulation, he seldom found his prayers answered these days.

'Why, what's the matter?' he asked, the excitement of having spotted a vacant spot inadvertently seeping into his voice. And it was barely a couple hundred steps away from his building block. Ronit had left work early today and if this was a reward for his timely arrival, he wasn't complaining.

'An incident in Mumbai... A high profile one. The target was RBG Holdings. Their CEO committed suicide this morning,' the caller explained.

'What! Isn't this Ramanathan's company... The guy who is married to the ex-minister's daughter?'

'Was married! Yes, it's the same guy... Apparently, he jumped off a bridge in Mumbai today.'

'Oh my God! Adhiraj, this can get really ugly,' Ronit replied. A frown had appeared on his forehead and his words were tinged with apprehension.

'It has started turning ugly already, Boss. The media is having a field day and the usual suspects are busy insinuating that this is an outcome of some elaborate government conspiracy to silence industrialists who oppose their agenda,' Adhiraj returned.

'Shit! This is bad news.'

'In all likelihood the case will land in our lap. So, to begin with, I am reaching out to the concerned agencies, requesting them to share the information that is currently available with them, and I will have a preliminary report ready for you by the time you reach office tomorrow,' Adhiraj said. 'Let me know in case you want me to explore any other angles as well.'

Ronit had reached his building and was about to climb the stairs: a section of the structure known for its tenuous relationship with mobile signals. He paused at the curtail step and said, 'That should be good to begin with. I am almost home… Let me get better understanding of the situation first and I will call you if anything else needs to be done. Otherwise, I will see you in office tomorrow morning.'

Ronit Biswas was a simple, bespectacled man in his mid-thirties. But veiled behind this humble exterior was a brilliant brain that had once been a prized target for many Silicon Valley majors. An alumnus of IIT Delhi and MIT, Ronit had already carved a name for himself in the field of Artificial Intelligence (AI) by the time he acquired his master's degree. He was still evaluating the many job offers he had landed when an unexpected phone call from the Indian Ambassador to The United States changed the trajectory of his life forever.

'Your country needs you,' were the four magic words that made all the difference.

The Indian government was planning to set up a new department for checking and preventing cybercrime within RAD (Research and Analysis Division), the country's premier intelligence agency. This was a pet project of the Home Minister, and he had personally sifted through the profiles of many successful Indian technocrats before zeroing in on Ronit. 'You understand the rapidly changing world of technology and your approach will be fresh and untainted,' the Ambassador had said, explaining the basis of the choice and inviting Ronit to set up and head this department.

To a Bengali boy with humble beginnings, the proposition was enough to propel his sense of patriotism into a different orbit. Despite mild resistance from Barkha, now his wife, Ronit returned to India and took up the job. Of course, the fact that he had been living in the US, away from her, for the past three years had a role to play in shaping his decision. The long-distance relationship had proven to be more strenuous than he had initially imagined, and he yearned to touch her, to hold her in his arms, to be with her. Ronit knew the importance of Barkha in his life, but her 'role' in shaping his career decision was something he would never acknowledge even to his own self.

'The next World War is not going to be fought by traditional weapons on borders as we know them, but through cyber weaponry—a few lines of code that can bring economies and governments to their knees. It is going to be a war of information, where countries will find themselves battling against invisible enemies in cyberspace… Imagine the things that a sixteen-year-old with an internet connection sitting on his couch in Islamabad can do today! Hell, he can bring an entire government down armed only with a laptop and an internet connection… And that is why we need you. We need your expertise to set up a team that will be at the core of our evolving defense strategy… We can't afford to be caught with our pants down when the time comes,' the Home Minister had said while inducting Ronit into RAD.

Ronit and his team—his deputies, Adhiraj and Myra, and a dozen analysts—had achieved several triumphs since then. From busting cyber scams to preventing phishing attacks, they had done it all over the years. But the job, which had been a joyride initially, was now becoming something of an irritant for Ronit. No matter how hard they worked or what cyber puzzles they were able to solve, it seemed that they were always falling short on the expectations of their political masters.

With changes in the political leadership, the very premise on which the Department of Cybercrime at RAD had been set up had undergone multiple iterations. Bureaucratic tussles and budget cuts had impaired the department's ability to stay abreast with technological advancements, while their invisible enemies were constantly upgrading their arsenal. This Ronit could still live with, but not the irrational and sometimes annoying demands and expectations of the political brass.

Most of them did not understand the basic differences between traditional crime and cybercrime. The fact that a cybercriminal could be sitting anywhere across the globe and could route an attack that was impossible to track, somehow became extremely difficult for Ronit to explain when something went wrong. Most hackers were lone wolves who did not leave an intelligence footprint like traditional criminals did, making it virtually impossible to pre-empt or prevent such attacks. Hence, most of the team's time went behind tracking and attempting to expose perpetrators of crimes once they had been committed. Sadly, the political elite viewed this as a sign of inefficiency and mediocrity.

Ronit knew that he wasn't soaring on the minister's popularity charts, and he didn't mind that to the slightest. What irked him most was men with little or no knowledge about his domain chiding his work and in words that often breached the frontiers of civility. The situation often made him wonder if the decision to leave a promising corporate career to come and work for a bunch of ignorant politicians had been a wise one.

Not very long ago, a senior member of the ruling party had summoned Ronit and asked him to use *computers* to figure out the precise location of an ancient treasure that was buried somewhere within the expanse of his constituency. The politician had received the tip from a godman, which obviously made it infallible. After he had spent a major portion of his allocated Local Area Development Fund in commissioning random and fruitless excavations across the district, he had decided to turn to technology for help. And Ronit, if the politician was to be believed, had come highly recommended.

It had taken Ronit all his intellect to explain to the man that computers were inept at performing what he believed to be a simple task. The man finally gave in, but not before he expressed his displeasure at Ronit's *uncooperative* attitude. Ronit's exasperation, as he stepped out of the meeting, had known no bounds.

As Ronit approached his third floor flat, he could feel a nervous weight building inside his belly. If what Adhiraj had said was true, and there was no reason for it not to be, he was staring at a difficult week ahead. Ramanathan's death would certainly be blown into a political scandal by the opposition, especially since one of their leaders was the deceased's father in-law.

And if indeed a cyber attack was found to have triggered it, Ronit would have to drastically expand his ability to absorb expletives over the coming days. The monthly review meeting of RAD department heads with the Home Minister was scheduled in four days, and the minister wasn't going to find a better reason to show Ronit his place.

Ronit raised his index finger towards ring the doorbell but paused midway. He pulled up his eyebrows and took a long breath, as though bracing himself for another unexpected blow, before letting the finger land.

CHAPTER 3

The Fallout

New Delhi, 4th August 2020

'Hi,' Ronit said, slipping past Barkha. To an onlooker, this might have appeared to be an expeditious greeting of a tired husband returning home to his wife of several years, but it really was Ronit attempting to escape the noxiousness permeating their marriage. He was like a student avoiding the teacher's eye while slipping inside the classroom, hoping to avoid being called out. Limiting his interactions with her to the perfunctory was Ronit's way of promoting peaceful cohabitation.

'You are back early…,' she returned after him.

'It was a relatively light day today,' he replied. 'So far…,' he added, claiming the remote and depositing himself on the sofa chair facing the television. Barkha walked back into the kitchen without offering a response.

'...MPTV has exclusive access to the voice message that C K Ramanathan had sent to his wife, Supriya, moments before taking the fatal plunge from the Vashi bridge. Viewers, please listen to the painful parting words of the deceased business tycoon and we will return to our panel of experts and hear their views on what might have pushed him over the edge.'

'You will have tea, right?' Barkha called out from the kitchen.

'Uh, yes please…,' Ronit responded, without taking his eyes off the television screen.

'Let us look at the facts as we know them,' the news anchor was back on the screen after the audio message had been played twice. 'C K Ramanathan had singlehandedly build a large retail empire, RBG Holdings, in less than two decades. Only last year he had been recognised among the top emerging business leaders of India by a renowned international publication. It is shocking that a man who was at the helm of an empire valued at over Rs 2,000 crores would end his own life so unceremoniously,' the anchor spoke as file pictures of Ramanathan's glory days played in a loop on the screen.

'India seeks answers... The country wants to know the real reason behind a successful business leader taking such a drastic and shocking step. So, let me cut across to our first guest, Arshi Sheikh of the LJP, for her opening remarks. Ms Sheikh, C K Ramanathan was married to the daughter of a senior leader of your party... He was not only successful professionally, but had a happy family with two schoolgoing children. What do you think is responsible for this disaster?'

'Afsha, we all know that the government of the day has been misusing central agencies to silence voices of its critics. This is all a big conspiracy, and today the country has paid a heavy price for turning a blind eye to their misconduct by losing a bright and promising business icon…,' Arshi had only started delivering her well-rehearsed opening lines when another panelist jumped in and started speaking over her.

'Do you people know anything other than to make baseless and false allegations? Didn't you hear what the Mumbai Police Commissioner said during his press conference?' he was yelling.

'Mr Rana, you will get your turn to speak… Please let Ms Sheikh complete what she is saying,' the anchor was forced to interrupt in a bid to maintain sanity in the discussion for as long as she could. It was going to be a difficult task though, considering the entrenched political differences between the panel members Ronit could see on the screen. Television debates had become an arena for verbal slugfests lately and Ronit detested them. He usually preferred online aggregators for his daily dose of news, but today was anything but usual.

'Tea,' Barkha said, placing one cup in front of him and relegating herself to the adjacent chair. 'Were you able to call the washing machine guys? How long before they are going to send a mechanic?' she said, reaching out for the TV remote.

'No, I need to watch this,' Ronit stopped her with a wave of his hand, his eyes still glued to the screen. 'They are short of manpower due to the pandemic. They have promised to send a mechanic as soon as they can,' he added.

'And what am I expected to do then? Manage, just like I am managing everything else in this house,' she murmured, withdrawing her outstretched hand. By now Ronit had learnt to identify the traps concealed in her words and steer clear of them. He refrained from offering a counter.

Ronit and Barkha's marital relationship had been another unexpected casualty of Ronit's career choices. They were both studying when they first met through a common friend many years back. He had been pursuing his undergraduate degree course from IIT, while Barkha was studying commerce at a Delhi University college. It had been a classic case of opposites attracting, and the effervescent and bubby Barkha was soon madly in love with the shy and reserved Ronit. To him, it was as if he had found a life beyond books and computer screens in Barkha.

Theirs was a perfect relationship which was meant to go all the way, and it did. When he decided to move to the US for further studies, Barkha assured him that they would make the long-distance relationship work, and they did. And when, in just over a year of his joining RAD, they decided to tie the nuptial knot, it surprised no one.

It was a few years into the marriage, when the initial sheen of their conjugal romance had begun to settle, when Ronit realised that the glue that bound them together was fast losing its viscosity. They were no longer the two people who had fallen deeply in love and decided to devote their entire lives to each other. He, for one, had changed tracks to becoming a very different person from the high-flying software guru he was meant to be. He was now a government servant, a spy to be precise, who had a taxing job that did not pay even a fraction of the money that his contemporaries in the private sector were making.

On the other hand, Barkha had always been a woman of the world driven by material wants and desires. She had let her dreams be known to him early on in their relationship. Ronit had seen the talk of international vacations, fancy cars and expensive brands bring a sparkle to young Barkha's eyes, and he had secretly fantasised about placing all these luxuries at her feet someday.

He was well on track to making their dreams a reality until a complex surge of emotions had derailed him. And now, whenever she saw pictures of Bali or Santorini bashfully posted on social media by her friends, Ronit noticed a cocktail of envy, disappointment and forced compromise in her dreamy eyes.

They weren't exactly struggling to make ends meet, but what they had was a normal middle-class life at best. A life that warranted prioritisation and planning, even when it came to making purchases like a new washing machine. It was Ronit who had failed Barkha and crushed her dreams, or so he believed.

Barkha had never confronted him on the matter, but

he had watched it gradually erode the joy and happiness that had once been the hallmark of their relationship. She smiled a lot less these days and often he found her words to be uncharacteristically caustic and piercing. The two were like a pair of frogs sitting in a pot of water, which had been put on the stove to boil. The heat around them was rising, but not abruptly enough for either of them to act on preventing the inevitable. Ronit found himself further fettered into inaction by the weight of his own guilt.

'...the police claim that the Enforcement Directorate (ED) received anonymous email tips—and mind you, not one but several emails—purportedly containing documentary proof of illegal transactions carried out by Mr Ramanathan on behalf of RBG Holdings, which prompted them to open an enquiry into the company and its promoter. I wish to ask Mr Rana if the ED even thought about ascertaining the veracity of these documents before opening their enquiry? And did they even try to find out the identity of this so-called whistleblower? Does the ED spring into action so swiftly to investigate every anonymous email that it receives?' the politician, Ms. Sheikh, was screaming at the top of her voice.

'Madam… Madam… It was only an investigation,' Rana interrupted her. 'If the ED doesn't investigate the complaint, how will they ever find out if the documents were authentic? And if Mr Ramanathan wasn't involved in anything illegal, he had absolutely nothing to worry about. He should have simply cooperated with the authorities. Doesn't his action prove that he had something to hide?'

'Mind your words Mr Rana! You have no right to vilify the deceased… It is not up to you or your party to pass a judgement on his character,' she burst out like a grenade having lost its pin. 'It wasn't just the ED… The Income Tax Department had also sent notices to C K Ramanathan. Isn't it odd that two central agencies should decide to investigate the same person at one time? Mr Rana, even a four-year-old can see what your government is up to. His blood is on your hands and your hands only.'

'Madam, didn't you hear what the police commissioner said? The IT department has documents in its possession that prove Ramanathan's involvement in tax fraud…'

'Oh please,' Arshi interjected animatedly. 'How do you think that so many confidential documents—some, which even the company management does not have access to—decided to turn up in the mailboxes of ED and IT officials? You will say that someone on the inside might have leaked them. But if the documents are indeed genuine, they would implicate anybody else who had access to them. That debunks this theory entirely… Afsha, the reality is that either these so-called documents don't exist, or they have been fabricated, and the ED and IT department used them to target and vilify an honest and law-abiding citizen of the country. Mr Rana might not understand this, but there are people in this world for whom their honour and dignity mean everything. And when Mr Ramanathan found the very foundations on which he had built his business empire under attack, he couldn't take it…'

As he watched the panellists emphatically make their points, the creases on Ronit's forehead continued to deepen. The opposition was clearly leaving no holds barred to corner the government on Ramanathan's suicide. This meant that the Home Minister would want answers from him, and soon. Ronit wondered if the Ramanathan's father-in-law had given his consent for making a spectacle of Ramanathan's death for the sake of scoring some political points. But he was quick to brush the thought aside. He had never understood the world of politics, and he was only glad that he had managed to keep himself distanced from it thus far.

'Adhiraj,' Ronit said, when the call was received.

'Yes, Boss,' he heard the youngster's harried voice in response.

'Listen, this appears to be more potent than I thought. We might have to get to the bottom of this quickly. Will you be able to leave for Mumbai tonight?'

'Tonight?'

'Yes! Why, is there a problem?'

'No… No problems, Boss,' Adhiraj replied. 'Just that the request was too sudden… Anyways, yes, I can take the late evening flight.'

'Good, do that! I will have a word with the Police Commissioner in the meantime and have someone meet you at the airport. I want you to join the investigations and figure out the source of the leaked documents. Check the company servers and Ramanathan's personal devices for traces of any malware that might have been used to hack the systems… I just hope that it was an insider and not some hacker who was responsible for the leaks…'

'I agree, Boss,' Adhiraj returned. 'I will get on with my travel bookings immediately.'

'Also, please speak to Myra and bring her up to speed on the matter. Keep her updated on whatever developments happen in Mumbai… I need to know them on a real time basis.'

'Sure Boss,' Adhiraj said, before disconnecting the call. Returning the phone to the bedside table, he rolled back to embrace the person lying beside him, half wrapped in a white cotton sheet. 'You heard… there go our evening plans… But I do have to bring you up to speed on something before that. The Boss's orders, after all,' he said, pinning her to bed and craning his neck forward.

'You know, your job, your boss and you, all suck,' Myra returned with feigned annoyance, before depositing her lips on his.

Chapter 4

The Bigger Picture

New Delhi, 8th August 2020

Ronit placed his bag in the scanner, lifted his identity card to eye level for the security guard's perusal and nodded in response to the greeting as he stepped through the walk-in metal detector at the entrance of the ministry building.

The building with its sandstone façade, majestic columns, remarkably high ceilings and the bustle of hectic energy, never ceased to intimidate him. The ministry and other vital government complexes in its vicinity made up the pulsating fulcrum of Indian democracy. This was where the architects of the country's future deliberated and planned their strategies. Ronit had been frequenting this place for several years—for his review meetings with the ministry officials, and otherwise when summoned—but he couldn't avoid feeling overwhelmed each time he stepped inside the ministry building.

As he took the lift to the second level, he continued to

rehearse the responses he had prepared for the questions that the Minister was likely to bury him under. Four days had passed since Ramanathan's death and they were far from solving the mystery enveloping it. Adhiraj had returned from Mumbai just the previous evening, and his report had only added to Ronit's miseries.

'The RBG server was hacked for sure, but I don't know how… The team is dissecting every program file for any suspicious codes as we speak, but at a cursory level I didn't find anything that could have been remotely fed into the server to secure access. My guess would be that the hacker somehow plugged into the company network and breached the server firewalls to access the files he was after… And I am guessing so only because the other alternative is way more farfetched. If indeed a hacker managed to enter the system remotely, it had to be the job of someone skilled enough to erase all traces of their intrusion as they left. This is not simple, since the malware codes would have to run across all storage systems connected to the server, and erasing all of them would be akin to removing a bundle of needles from a haystack without missing out on a single one. I don't know many Indian hackers who are capable of accomplishing such a feat,' Adhiraj had summarised his findings.

Ronit had no reasons to doubt his deputy's assessment. Adhiraj was as capable an expert in his field as any, and if he was suggesting that C K Ramanathan had fallen prey to an anonymous hacking attack, that had to be the truth. Only, the information had left Ronit in a bit of a quandary, for he had to attend the monthly review with the Minister the next morning. He had been hoping that Adhiraj's investigations would yield something substantive, if not a breakthrough, which would help him save face in front of the minister. With his solitary ray of hope brutally extinguished, he had no option but to brace for the worst.

Ronit could feel an apprehensive tremble in his hands as he turned the knob to open the heavy wooden door leading to the conference room. The room he stepped into was a bit of a contrast to a stereotypical conference facility. With plush carpets, heavy mahogany furniture and a glass chandelier dangling from the ceiling, it reeked of old-world opulence. But for the oval desk in its centre and the dozen odd chairs surrounding it, the room could have passed for the living room of a heritage bungalow.

On one end of the room was a snack counter, where a uniformed butler was handing out cups of tea and coffee to the attendees. Ronit spotted Vikrant Yadav, Chief of the Department of International Affairs at RAD, engaged in a conversation with the Home Secretary.

'Hello RB… Good morning,' the Home Secretary, Mr Gupta, responded to Ronit's greeting as he approached the duo. Vikrant chimed in with a gruff, inaudible greeting of his own.

'Hello Mr Yadav,' Ronit repeated, eliciting another response from his colleague, albeit not very different from the previous one. 'So, as I was saying… this is the second such incident in recent times and Malaysia remains reluctant to even consider revisiting in their stance. The Chinese are obviously further emboldened by this and who knows what they will try next. We have no option but to sit on the sidelines and watch them expand their hegemony in the region,' Yadav, ignoring Ronit's presence, resumed his conversation with the Home Secretary.

Ronit held his ground obstinately. Yadav was a seasoned bureaucrat, within striking distance of his retirement. He had grown through the ranks, proving his worth time and again to reach the pivotal position he held at RAD now. The International Affairs department of RAD was the liaison office between RAW, India's overseas intelligence gathering agency, which operated under the aegis of the Ministry of External Affairs, and the multitude of domestic intelligence and law enforcement bodies. Yadav and his team were responsible for recognising and thwarting threats to the Indian mainland or its residents based on global intelligence. Basing his knowledge of some of the terror plots that the team had foiled in the past, Ronit knew that many Indian citizens, who perhaps owed their lives to the bravehearts working in this department, did not even know about its existence.

However, Yadav was a man plagued with his own idiosyncrasies. For him, youth and academic qualifications were not a worthy substitute for experience, and his displeasure at Ronit's appointment as his peer at RAD had been overt and consistent. But Ronit didn't seem to mind. The old man was one of the few people at RAD who spoke their mind openly, and Ronit respected this trait. Of course, Yadav's understanding of intelligence and the clandestine networks he had laboriously built over the years were unparalleled and Ronit could think of no better person to manage International Affairs than him.

'We were talking about the recent incident in the South China Sea,' Gupta, noticing the look of confusion on Ronit's face, clarified.

'What incident?' Ronit quizzically returned. He had been too preoccupied with preparing for the meeting to remain abreast with global news stories. No sooner had the words escaped his lips, he realised the error he had made.

'The incident in the South China Sea… You haven't heard of it? Which rock are you living under?' Yadav was quick to take a jab.

'A Chinese survey ship, HD-6 had entered Malaysian waters last evening. Apparently, it ventured perilously close to a Malaysian oil exploration vessel. The standoff lasted several hours before the Chinese finally withdrew. Expectedly, the Malaysian authorities have refused to formally comment on the matter,' Gupta, meaning to contain an escalation of an entirely different nature, explained.

The SCS or South China Sea is a region of tremendous economic and geostrategic importance, with nearly a third of global maritime shipping passing through it. The lucrative fisheries and huge oil and natural gas reserves beneath its seabed lend considerable pecuniary value to the SCS. Consequently, the South China Sea islands, comprising hundreds of uninhabited atolls, reefs and shoals, have been witnessing competing claims of sovereignty from countries like Philippines, Vietnam, Taiwan, Indonesia, Malaysia and China.

Given China's aggressive stance and machinations to gain control of the region, several world powers including the United States, Japan, Australia and India have time and again stood up to its dominant behaviour, pushing for resolution of the prevailing conflicts. These countries have maintained that their merchant and naval ships have historically sailed unhindered through the South China Sea and they would continue to do so. Ronit was aware that over the past few months, China had been taking advantage of the distraction offered by the coronavirus pandemic to advance its presence in the region.

'The Malaysians are continuing to toe the Chinese line, as expected… But we have tabled a proposal for a joint naval exercise to Australia and Japan. Some other ASEAN nations might participate as well. This should help us keep check on the Chinese for now,' Yadav responded. His words were directed at the Home Secretary, a man who could serve as a crucial ally for Yadav when the matter came up for discussions later. He hadn't even bothered to glance at Ronit as he spoke.

'Perhaps the Panda Diplomacy carries more weight than one would like to believe,' Ronit pitched in, leaning on his extant knowledge of the matter to contribute to the conversation.

China, which possesses virtually all the giant pandas on earth, has been using the lovable bears as an expression of friendship and to further its diplomatic ties with other nations since the cold war era. Between 1957 and 1983, 24 pandas were gifted by China to nine nations including USA, UK, USSR and Korea as a gesture of friendship. Subsequently, the Chinese policy was modified to permit pandas to be given to other nations only as long-term loans and not as gifts. In 2014, Malaysia was the proud recipient of a pair of giant pandas—Feng and Fu—on loan for a period of ten years.

'If animals are what it takes for them to shape their foreign policies, I don't mind sending them a container full of mules and buffaloes from here… We have plenty of those meandering on the streets…,' Yadav responded irritably, finally acknowledging Ronit's presence. Gupta and Ronit burst out laughing at the way the veteran had wrinkled his nose while delivering the punch.

Just then the conference room door burst open and the minister's hassled-looking assistant scampered in. This meant that the man himself wasn't far behind. The incessant chatter in the room abruptly ceased, and Ronit, Yadav and Gupta, just like the others, rushed to occupy their designated seats. Within moments the room was ready for the minister's arrival.

The first topic to come up for discussions was the recent Chinese intrusion in the South China Sea. Ronit was happy to sit back and observe as Yadav nervously updated the minister on the evolving situation. The incident, unlike the demise of C K Ramanathan, was relatively fresh and the group was curious to learn more. Given China's increasing commercial influence and the blow-hot-blow-cold relationship that the two militaries shared on India's northern borders, the minister too was liberal with his questions. After all, when it came to China, one could never be sure as to which actions might have what reactions and where.

Ronit watched his veteran colleague dig into all his experience and expertise to deftly navigate through the queries flung at him. Only towards the end of the scheduled time did the minister shift his attention away from Yadav and towards Ronit.

'Have we got any breakthrough on the Ramanathan case yet?' he said without bothering with niceties.

'Sir, we have been actively participating in the probe, and all that we can say with certainty at this point is that the RBG Holdings' servers were hacked. The hacker appears to have gained access to a variety of confidential company documents including the ones that were leaked to ED and Income Tax department. We are working on ascertaining the identity of the hacker and should have some positive news soon…'

'Mr Biswas,' the minister interjected. His face looked as though he had just gulped down a glass of bitter gourd juice. 'I thought technology was meant to help us get things done faster… Here we are, four days after a crime was committed, and you are telling me that you are still working on identifying the perpetrator? I don't know if you have noticed, but the issue is fast spiralling out of hand… God knows how you can be so apathetic and lax on the matter…'

Ronit's eyes were affixed on the notepad in front of him as he ingested the minister's words. He knew from experience that the lesser he spoke the better it was for him. But he was forced to look up when the minister paused to stare at him.

'Yes, sir… I understand,' he murmured.

'You understand nothing…,' the minister retorted, raising his voice slightly. 'The opposition is freely peddling their own narrative and we are doing nothing to control it. Do you know how the markets are reacting to the insinuation that the government is misusing federal agencies to jeopardise business entities? The BSE Sensex, which was already reeling under the impact of the pandemic, has further lost almost two thousand points since this news broke. Do you even know how much monetary loss that translates into for the common investors?'

'Yes, sir…'

'Don't just sit here and *yes-sir* me… I need results and I need them soon. And while your investigations are on, deploy some people to control the misinformation campaign that is being run on social media. Bloody, everyday thousands of new accounts are springing up out of nowhere and spreading lies about how the government is responsible for this man's death. *Arey*, it wasn't we who pushed him down the bridge, did we?'

'No, sir…'

'Of course, we did not!' the minister shot out yet again. Ronit bit his tongue, realising that the question was purely rhetorical, and it didn't call for an answer. 'Now, will you look into this personally and ensure that the damage is contained immediately?'

'Yes, sir…,' he said, after a hesitant pause.

The meeting hadn't gone well for Ronit, but he had endured far worse in the past. As he made for the elevator lobby, Ronit could only thank the Chinese for the distraction they had unwittingly provided. He had survived the day and now he had time by his side. A plan was already forming in his head, and he felt a lot more confident about containing the situation soon.

Chapter 5

Beyond The Borders

Kuala Lumpur, Malaysia, 14th October 2020

It was an unadorned room with bare brick walls where the girl, dressed in a black tank top and slacks was landing powerful jabs, punches and kicks on the heavy leather bag dangling from a hook on the ceiling. But for the few dumbbells and exercise equipment strewn around, the room was virtually empty. It was a small room with acoustics that weren't designed for the use it was being put to. The thuds, each time she landed a punch or a kick, and her piercing shrieks lingered in the air, lending a rugged, intense feel to the place.

When her phone announced an incoming text message, she paused to glare at it. The handset was placed on the floor near the door along with her sipper and hand towel. If the phone had been *smart* enough to sense and decipher her look, it most certainly would have opted to play dead.

She reached out for her towel and sipper first, dabbed the perspiration from her face and took a swig of water before claiming the phone. A swipe of the screen revealed the message that had interrupted her intense early morning routine.

'We got a hit,' was all that the message said. Instead of the sender's name or phone number, the words *Private Number* were displayed above the message. This didn't seem to surprise her though. She knew the source of the message perfectly well and her lips curled ever so slightly as she read it. She had been waiting for this news for a long time. Perhaps her wait of many months was going to end now.

She opened the door and stepped into what looked like the living room of a small apartment. The furnishings were modern and tasteful, but the random garments flung across the couch and the empty utensils resting on the corner table did not speak very highly of the occupant's housekeeping skills. She crossed the room without a pause and made straight for the bedroom.

When she emerged ten minutes later, she had transformed into an entirely different person. Dressed in a cotton shirt and black pants, with a tudung (headscarf) wrapped around her head and neck, she looked no different than the hundreds of working women who flocked the business districts of KL. Her demeanour too, as she left the apartment, was far more subdued than the girl who had been mercilessly pounding on the punching bag a short while back.

'Selamat pagi, Madam,' the security guard greeted her, drawing her from her reverie. She paused to smile at him, before approaching the retina scanner. There was a spring in her steps as she strode across the granite floor to approach the reception desk.

'Good morning, Noor,' the lady at the reception said. Pointing to the corridor on her left, she added, 'Meeting room three.'

'Thanks, Farah,' Noor returned, before proceeding in the indicated direction. Noor Sabah looked several years younger than the twenty-eight years she had already navigated mother earth. She had an innocent, smooth face resting on a fit but petite frame. Early in her life she had learnt to use her looks to evoke strong paternal instincts in the men she encountered. This augured well in Noor's chosen line of work. Of course, she had also trained herself adequately to transform into a coldblooded, ruthless killer at will.

Noor Sabah was a rising star in the game of international espionage. She was one of Malaysia's finest: one of the country's most valuable secret service agents.

'Good morning, Major,' she said, wishing the hard-faced man sitting at the head of the table. The Major had been scratching his beard with one hand, his head tilted ever so slightly, and eyes resting on nothing in particular. Noor knew him well enough to tell that he was in deep contemplation. Major Taufiq was Noor's handler, the man who had drawn her to the office with his cryptic message. 'Good morning,' she added for the benefit of other occupants of the room. Noor didn't recognise any of the other three men. These were the nameless, faceless analysts who worked behind the scenes to provide the likes of Noor the ammunition they needed to succeed in their work. And if the Major's message was anything to go by, they might have just achieved the impossible.

'Come, Noor,' the Major replied, directing her to an adjacent chair with his hand. 'It seems we finally have a breakthrough… Why don't one of you show her what you've got?'

A bespectacled young man got up from his chair at the Major's command. 'Sure, Sir. Hello, Madam, I am Aseef from the analysis wing,' he began, twiddling his thumb nervously.

'So, as you know, we have been tracking Zhiming's movements with the aim of finding her in a neutral geography where it is feasible for us to establish contact with her. This has been a herculean task on multiple counts. First, we don't have adequate information or even a clear photograph of her—other than the two dated and grainy pictures—making it difficult to track her. And then, from what we know, she is adept at keeping her presence masked in the physical as well as the cyber world. Therefore, we were able to get just two hits on her over the past eight months, one of which turned out to be a false alarm and the other placed her in Beijing, her home turf.'

Noor was aware of the efforts and challenges faced by the team tasked with tracking Zhiming. Zhiming, a mandarin name which roughly translated to *lethal* or *deadly*, was more of an epithet that the Major had bestowed upon the elusive Chinese secret agent. Neither Malaysian intelligence nor the Interpol were aware of her real identity. The two images that they had in their possession, they believed to be of Zhiming, based purely on circumstantial evidence. They could very well have been expending their energy in tracking a common Chinese citizen all this while.

It had been nine months since the Major had briefed Noor and handed over the case file to her. She was aghast at what she had learnt and there was little doubt that this was going to be the most decisive cases that she had handled so far. In fact, the future of her country rested on Zhiming being apprehended and made to sing their tune.

While the Major had tasked a team of analysts to continuously comb cyberspace in search of Zhiming, Noor had set out to locate her using her own means. However, she had little to show for all her efforts so far. In fact, the false lead that the analyst Aseef had just referred to had also been pursued by Noor. It had taken her on a wild goose chase to Hong Kong and then Singapore, where she had finally realised that she had been running behind the wrong target. The woman she had been chasing was an expensive escort with a clientele comprising affluent men of notable social stature. She bore a very fleeting resemblance to the Zhiming of their pictures, and that was her only perceivable link to the world of covert operations.

Noor was eager to learn about the latest discovery that the team had made, and she was hoping that Aseef would conclude his preamble soon and get to the relevant part. However, she refrained from interrupting him or letting her impatience show.

'A few months back, we noticed certain incidents in India which had been executed in a manner quite similar to Zhiming's known modus operandi. So, we focused our efforts in trying to track her there. We set up multiple alerts, including an alert on the video feeds of important transit points in the country. Now, this would have been impossible under normal circumstances due to the heavy traffic of commuters. Our facial recognition software would have taken weeks to scan the images captured in just a single day, but the reduced traffic on account of the pandemic made it worth a try... And now it appears that our gamble has finally paid off. Here, this is what the system sounded an alert for,' he said, pointing the remote towards the screen.

Two images of the same woman came up on screen. The first was a side capture where she could be seen entering an airport terminal, and the second was a frontal closeup taken near what looked like a boarding gate.

'These pictures are from the Mumbai airport from two days back, and they are ninety two percent match with her photographs on our file. If this is indeed her, she has taken a flight from Mumbai to Delhi two days back. We have increased our bandwidth allocation for scanning the security feeds from the Delhi airport, but a match is yet to show up,' Aseef explained.

'Let me put up both set of photographs for comparison,' he added, bending on his laptop. As he played with the keyboard, the screen went blank and then came alive once again. There were four pictures visible now—the two pictures from Mumbai airport and two other pictures which were relatively grainy and obscure. But it didn't require a genius to conclude that all four photographs belonged to the same woman.

'It is her,' Noor muttered without taking her eyes off the screen.

'Yes, it looks like we finally have the elusive Zhiming within our grasp,' Major Taufiq concurred.

'So, how do we approach this now?' Noor asked, locking her eyes with the Major's.

'Well, you need to head to Delhi, locate her and somehow get her to give you what we want… Simple, isn't it?' the Major responded with an uncharacteristic grin. Perhaps permitting himself the liberty of a wisecrack was his way of celebrating the achievement.

'Yes, simple indeed,' Noor returned. 'But we do have a few challenges to consider first… For instance, how will I get into India? Aren't they still persisting with their ban on international flights?'

'Given the nature of this case I don't think you need to worry about such trivialities. You can travel to Delhi in a private aircraft, or better still, a military plane. We will get all the necessary clearances that are needed,' the Major replied. 'In fact, we will inform the Indian

Ambassador that we are stationing a medical team in our Delhi embassy as a first line of treatment for coronavirus infections that our staff or their family members might contract. The count of cases in the city has been rising steadily and their medical infrastructure is under extreme stress. They will have no reason to deny such a request. You can go there as a part of this medical team… It will serve as the perfect cover for you.'

'But India is our ally. Why do we need to play this cat and mouse game with them? Why can't we simply read them in on this and seek their cooperation instead?'

'For starters, we don't know if Zhiming is indeed in Delhi, and if she is, what she is doing there. If we approach the Indian authorities at this stage, they are bound to pose questions that we will not have answers to. Hence, it will be more prudent for us to initiate the investigation on our own. You will have our agent network in India at your disposal, and the Malaysian Ambassador will have specific instructions to provide you with all the support you need.'

Noor responded with an understanding nod.

'While the decision to subsequently involve the Indians rests with you and the Ambassador, I will recommend against it unless absolutely necessary. If the Indian authorities were to mount a manhunt to nab Zhiming, it might tip her off. And that is not something we can afford. If we lose her this time, who knows when we will manage to catch her scent again.'

'I get it,' Noor replied. 'I will make sure that we

succeed in this operation, no matter what it takes.'

'Your country expects no less from you, Noor. Now let us set the ball rolling and see how soon we can have you on your way to India,' the Major said, getting up from his chair.

This was a cue for the analysts to make an exit. They folded their wares and quietly slipped out of the room without even waiting for an acknowledgement of the miraculous feat that they had achieved. Neither of them knew the importance of this operation for their country, but they could sense from the conversation that they had made a noteworthy contribution towards something big and significant.

Chapter 6

A Brief Distraction

New Delhi, 18th October 2020

Ronit Biswas had come in early today and he had been glued to his laptop for the past couple of hours. If the creases on his forehead and the Starbucks takeaway cup filled with what had once been steaming coffee, lying on his table were anything to go by, he wasn't having the best of days.

And this time it wasn't work. Ronit and his team had successfully managed to avert the crisis that had been brewing on account of C K Ramanathan's untimely demise. Although the hacker remained at large, they were successful in strongarming the two major social media platforms into blocking thousands of accounts that were using the businessman's suicide to peddle a narrative against the present dispensation. Ronit as well as the company representatives knew that most of these were fake accounts run by agencies on opposition payrolls to dispense stories favourable to them and troll those who posted opposing viewpoints. Therefore, it had been relatively easy to arrive at an understanding with them.

These accounts were blocked in batches and suddenly it seemed as if the country had lost interest in the case and moved on. Traditional media channels were quick to take cue and shift their focus to more pertinent stories. Interested parties got no time to bolster their depleted ranks and revive the issue on social media, and just like that, the story of Ramanathan's demise was relegated to the archives as a tragic and sad happening. The matter had been contained and that is all the Minister seemed to care about.

'Boss,' Adhiraj, who had just opened the door to his cabin and stepped inside, interrupted Ronit. 'We are going to bring the boy in now. I just thought I will let you know.'

'The boy?... oh, yes,' Ronit said, taking a brief pause to discern the context. 'Take Myra along; her soft touch might come in handy… And remember, no paperwork whatsoever. I want to meet him personally as soon as he gets here.'

'Sure, Boss,' Adhiraj said, before making an exit.

The boy in question was a seventeen-year-old high school student who had hacked into Google's servers and changed their homepage Doodle into an animated caricature of an Indian cricketer thrashing a Pakistani player with his bat. Ronit, like millions of other Google users had seen the Doodle but failed to take note of it at first. It was only when the story began to trend, and Google was forced to issue a press statement and file a formal complaint that he became aware of the mischief.

The miscreant might not have intended any harm other than to infuriate the sport aficionados across the border, but he had committed a crime, nonetheless. Ronit decided to investigate the matter, more out of curiosity than anything else. A hacker who could evade the firewalls of a tech giant such as Google was capable of much more. He could have hacked into somebody's bank account and made away with the money, or he could have breached a government server and gained access to confidential information. Ronit was perplexed as to why the hacker chose to go through so much trouble to do something that he could not benefit from in any way.

Although Adhiraj had been tasked with the investigation, Ronit had remained personally involved in it from the very beginning. He had closely monitored every tiny bit of progress, studying the hacker's modus operandi with great interest. The code that had been used to gain access to the company servers was unlike anything that Ronit had seen before. It was the Monalisa equivalent of a program code—fascinating and faultless. The code had only worked to further fuel Ronit's curiosity about the hacker.

They tried to locate the IP address from where the hack code had been uploaded, but the hacker was once again ahead of them. He had bounced his signals through multiple proxy servers across the globe, making it virtually impossible for them to zero in on his location.

Had it not been for a bizarre slip-up, there had been no way for them to identify the hacker.

The team discovered that it had taken the hacker two attempts to upload his code on the Google server. In the first attempt, only a fourth of the code had been uploaded before the hacker's connection to the server was abruptly severed. In a span of a few minutes the connection was back up again, and this time he succeeded in transferring the entire program without any interruptions.

'The security programs on the server couldn't detect the malware, so the disconnection wasn't triggered by them. It has to be something at the hacker's end, maybe a power failure, that interrupted the upload,' Adhiraj had concluded. Ronit could not think of a better explanation for the slipup either.

Only when the program started uploading for the second time did the source tracker ping a location in Noida before it resumed its routine of jumping from one country to another. The split-second it took for the program designed to conceal the source location of the code to kick in was enough for the digital forensic experts at RAD to pinpoint the location where the hack had been initiated from.

'Lovlesh Sharma, he is a Class 11 student,' Adhiraj disclosed the hacker's identity to Ronit, his brows pulled up in disbelief. This was last evening.

The team had then spent some time debating over the next steps on the matter. In normal course they would have handed over their findings to the local police or crime branch and let them handle the arrest and prosecution of the culprit. However, given the boy's age, neither Adhiraj nor Myra were in favor of handing him to the police. They knew that an arrest would not only sully his record for life, but it would also close several doors for him in the future. Ronit's deputies were hesitant of making the harsh call in a hurry.

'Okay, we will be well within our rights to summon him for questioning as part of the ongoing investigation. We don't need to call him out as a suspect yet,' Ronit suggested. This was one of the rare instances when Ronit had agreed to bend the rules he swore by, and for good reason. The kid's work stood testimony to his potential and Ronit didn't want to be the one to push him into an abyss that he would struggle to emerge from for the remainder of his life. It was thus agreed that Adhiraj would prepare a formal summon and bring the boy to RAD for questioning the next morning.

'Take one plainclothes constable from the local police station with you, just in case…,' Ronit had suggested. 'I will call the station incharge of the area and tell him to expect you tomorrow.'

Ronit had managed to stall the decision for now, but he was aware that the conundrum would spring up again once he had spoken with the kid. If the kid had committed the crime, and of this Ronit had little doubt, he would have to be charged as per the provisions of the law. Ronit would once again find himself grappling with the same questions that he had successfully evaded for the time being. And then, if he allowed his emotions to take charge, he would risk overstepping the boundaries of legality.

These conflicting thoughts from the previous evening came rushing back to Ronit as soon as Adhiraj left his cabin. It was now a matter of hours when he would have to choose between what the law of the land proclaimed to be right and what his heart believed to be so.

'Let's cross the bridge when we get to it,' he said out aloud to his own self. He then covered his face with his palms and used the first two fingers of each hand to massage his eyes. His head was throbbing, partly from the lack of sleep and partly under the burden of his own thoughts. When images from last night started playing within his head once again, Ronit made no attempt to stop them.

It was just before eight that Ronit had reached home. After ringing the bell twice, he realised that Barkha wasn't in. He assumed that she must have stepped out to buy groceries, and he used his set of keys to let himself in.

He waited patiently, but when an hour passed by without any signs of her, he started to get worried. It wasn't usual for Barkha to stay out so late, and he was aware that the neighborhood shops shut down early these days on account of the pandemic. He tried to call her, but the call went unanswered. The thought of calling her parents crossed his mind, but he decided against acting in haste. There was no point burdening them over what was probably nothing but his own overreaction.

He kept calling her number every ten minutes, only to be greeted by a long ring followed by a mechanical voice which informed him that the person he was trying to reach was not responding. As if he needed to be told that his wife was not only missing from home, but she wasn't taking his calls either. Ronit was somehow managing to keep dreadful thoughts from surfacing, but he could feel his trepidation mounting with each unanswered call..

It was a few minutes after his fourth or fifth attempt to reach her that the doorbell rang. He rushed to open it, banging his knee against the table corner in the process. He had to bite his lower lip to contain a scream.

'Where have you been?' he shot out as soon as he saw Barkha at the door.

'I was out to meet a friend,' she said, sidestepping him and making for the bedroom. 'Why? What happened?' Ronit thought he caught a whiff of beer on her breath. He followed her inside.

'You could have at least informed me. I called you multiple times, but you didn't pick up…'

'Oh, is it?' she said, reaching out for the phone in her handbag. This was when Ronit noticed that Barkha was fully decked up, clad in her favourite dress and wearing an unusually bold makeup. 'I am sorry, it was on silent…'

'Have you had dinner? I had left it in the kitchen…,' she asked nonchalantly, opening the wardrobe to extract her night clothes. 'I have had my dinner already… You go ahead and eat, and please put the extra food in the fridge,' she replied when he offered to bring her a plate too.

Shortly after they had retired to bed, Barkha's phone pinged, announcing the arrival of a text message. Although his eyes were shut, Ronit wasn't asleep yet. He could make out from her movements that Barkha had picked up her phone from the bedside table and switched off its ringer. The incoming messages did not stop though. From the sound of the phone vibrating against the wooden tabletop, Ronit could tell that she received four more messages within a span of two minutes. Someone was desperately trying to catch her attention. Perhaps Barkha had been eager to read the messages too, for she quietly picked up her phone and tiptoed into the bathroom. It was only after 20 long minutes that she emerged, clutching the phone in hand. Ronit did not hear the toilet flush behind her.

Seeds of suspicion had started rearing their ugly head in the already murky waters of their relationship. A part of Ronit knew that he should give her the benefit of the doubt, or perhaps confront her and offer her an opportunity to present her side of the story, but this sane voice was being eclipsed by random thoughts and emotions that seemed to have taken charge of his being. He couldn't prevent his thoughts from darting back to situations where Barkha's conduct had been atypical if not suspicious, and the cynical side of him was using these memories to bolster his misgivings about her and them. Ronit's fears were like a raging tornado, feeding on his memories to expand and acquire a devastating girth, and he found himself unable to contain them despite his best efforts.

'The boy is here, Boss. He's sitting in the ground floor meeting room. Do you want me to get him here?' This time it was Myra who had appeared to break the chain of his thoughts.

'No, I will come with you. It will be less intimidating for him there,' Ronit said, getting up from his seat to follow Myra.

'A middle-aged man intercepted them in the corridor leading to the meeting room. 'Sir...sir, I am Rakesh Sharma, Lovlesh's father. Your people have brought my son here and they are saying that you are going to question him regarding some crime,' he said. Possibly he knew that Myra had gone to summon her superior and he had been lying in wait to present his plea to the more competent authority.

'Sir, I teach in a school… we are simple people… my son can't be involved in any crime. This is a big mistake. Unlike most boys his age, Lovlesh doesn't even have many friends. He spends most of his time locked up in his room with a book or his computer. He is innocent,' the man said, folding his hands. Ronit could see a wet film appear on the white of his eyes. The man was on the brink of breaking into tears. 'Please save him, Sir… please…'

Ronit, who was already in an emotionally charged state, felt something twist within his belly. 'Don't worry,' he said, placing his hand on Rakesh Sharma's shoulder. 'Let me go and speak with him. It won't take long. And if he tells us what we want to know, you can take him back home with you.'

'Sir, please...,' the man persisted. Sniffing hard he continued, 'If he gets caught up in something untoward, it will destroy his future. If there is any way... anything that I can do... please tell me. I have some savings which I had put aside for his college education...' Rakesh let his words tail, his hands still folded and eyes searching Ronit's face for any clue on what he could do to protect his son.

'Mr Sharma, I told you, there's no need for you to worry. Keep your money and use it for the purpose you have been saving it for,' Ronit said, sidestepping the man and heading down the corridor.

As he entered the meeting room, Ronit caught sight of Lovlesh, sitting on a chair and looking like a sheep due for slaughter. He was a chubby boy, a connoisseur of his mother's butter-laden parathas perhaps, with unkempt hair and a freckled face. His t-shirt carried a dreadful print of zombie and skeleton images and was at least two sizes too big for him. He watched Ronit sit on the chair across him with expectant, fearful eyes.

'Lovlesh Sharma,' Ronit said, extracting a piece of paper from his jacket pocket. 'You know, coding is my passion too... and I must admit that the code you have written left me spellbound. I looked minutely for chinks in the program but could find none. Only, one small area of improvement,' he said, placing the paper in front of the boy. It had the program code used for the hack printed on it. 'Here, if you had closed this loop at this point, it would have given you the same result in a less circuitous manner. Not that it matters, but you could have saved yourself a few nanoseconds of processing time.'

The boy's expressions didn't change much on account of Ronit's spiel, but he did glance at the sheet of paper from the corner of his eye.

'We both know that you made a mistake, but that is not what I am here to discuss. Had that been my agenda, you would have been sitting inside a police station right now and not here. So, don't be scared,' Ronit persisted. 'I was curious to meet the person who wrote this flawless code, and my interest is to see if we can find a way to nurture the exceptional talent you possess. I am sure your father would be hoping for the same.'

'Can I get you something? Some coffee or water?' Ronit abruptly shifted gears. Lovlesh declined with a shake of the head, but he was looking much more at ease now.

'Okay, so here is what we can do… If you promise to stay out of mischief and focus on your studies, I can make all this go away. You can go back home with your father,' Ronit continued. 'I will also see if I can land you some freelance projects to keep you gainfully occupied. However, we will be monitoring every click of your keyboard, and our deal will be off the minute you make another mistake. No one will be able to save you from going to prison then… Does that make sense?'

'Yes, Sir,' the boy mumbled. As soon as the words escaped his mouth, his tear ducts gave way. Rivulets of tears ran down his cheeks and he broke into a soft, inaudible sob. Ronit waited for a few minutes before stepping around the table and placing his palm on the boy's head.

'I am sorry, Sir… It was a big mistake. I did it just for fun, to fulfill a challenge posted by someone on a dark web bulletin. I thought that it was a harmless prank, and I could earn some bitcoins by completing the challenge. It didn't even occur to me that my actions could have such far-reaching consequences. I promise, I will never engage in anything like this ever again,' he said in a quivering voice peppered with sobs and sniffs.

'Don't worry, making mistakes is only human. All of us have made our fair share of mistakes and continue to make them even today. What is important is to learn from them and ensure that they are not repeated. Go, your father is anxiously waiting to take you home.'

As Ronit returned to his cabin, laden with words of gratitude from Lovlesh and his father, he only hoped that his good deed would infuse some goodness into his own life. He had prevented a young boy's future from certain jeopardy, but his own life prospects seemed utterly gloomy and bleak.

Chapter 7

The Mysterious Invitation

New Delhi, 23rd December 2020

Ronit was a habitual early riser. He liked to get to office early and plan the rest of his day in advance. The peace and quiet preceding the clamour of a regular workday allowed him to structure his thoughts and prioritise among the issues that needed dealing with.

Today had been no different. Ronit had stopped at the regular coffee shop for his morning fix of latte, and clutching the paper cup, had driven with one hand for the next five minutes to swerve inside the RAD office complex. As he exited the lift and made for his cabin, he glanced around the floor. He could see three people on their workstations already, but none from his team. He was the first one to check in yet again.

He had barely spent about fifteen minutes in his cabin when Yadav barged in, demanding to have a word. Ronit was affronted enough to consider excusing himself and asking the veteran to send him a formal meeting request instead, but the urgency in Yadav's voice was palpable. The man anyways wasn't known for his polished ways, and so, Ronit decided to hear him out.

'I need your team to help me figure out something,' he began. His tone was uncertain, as if he were trying to decide on the right approach for seeking help from a man he didn't consider to be his equal. He couldn't afford to be overly condescending and yet he wasn't prepared to expose his vulnerabilities by adopting an utterly humble stance. Ronit had a feeling that he was going to enjoy the conversation.

'You are aware of the farmers' agitation, I hope?'

Ronit refrained from responding and looked Yadav straight in the eye. The derisive question was clearly Yadav overcompensating for his initial plea, and Ronit wasn't prepared to entertain this. For over a week the farmers' protest had been making headlines and anyone remotely connected with the goings-on in the country couldn't possibly be oblivious to it.

The central government had recently passed a set of three acts, commonly known as the Farm Bills, in a bid to help small and marginal farmers get better price for their produce and gain access to investments for boosting productivity. These laws allowed farmers to sell their produce outside of government run mandis or APMCs, thereby reducing their transportation costs and ushering benefits of competitive pricing for their crops. With the passage of the laws, farmers could enter into contracts with agri-business firms or large retailers to sell their produce at pre-determined rates.

However, farmer unions from certain northern states of the country where the mandi system was more established had been vocal about their reservations against the Bills. They feared that privatisation would lead to the dismantling of *mandis* and they would eventually lose the cushion of Minimum Support Price (MSP) that they enjoyed today. Their argument was that over time large corporate houses would begin to dictate terms and arm-twist farmers into accepting even lesser rates for their crops than they get today.

Expectedly, the opposition was leaving no stone unturned to corner the government of the day on this issue. Several political parties had pledged their support to farmers and demanded that these laws be repealed immediately. Their argument was that the government had hastily passed the bills without consultations or deliberations with relevant stakeholders, hinting at possible collusion with business houses that could potentially benefit from their passage.

Fueled by political backing and media attention, the voices of dissent had grown into a protest and were now threatening to blow up into a full-scale agitation. Though Ronit hadn't actively educated himself on the matter, he was adequately versed with its broad contours.

'Okay, so we have reasons to believe that certain vested interest groups might be trying to hijack the agenda of the agitation,' Yadav was forced to break the uncomfortable silence. 'It seems that some separatist and leftist groups have joined hands with sections of protesting farmers, and they are not only funnelling money into the agitation but are also trying to reestablish their foothold in the country through this.'

'I have heard speculations to this effect too, but nothing concrete so far,' Ronit chimed in. His interest in Yadav's oratory had started to grow.

'That is because the protesting farmers are not a single entity. They comprise several dozen organised unions, non-governmental organisations (NGOs) and lakhs of individual landowners. In such a scenario, it is virtually impossible to differentiate the ill-motivated ones from genuine protestors. And with the sympathy wave going for them, we can't even afford to round up those who have been known supporters of these fringe groups in the past. That can go horribly wrong in more ways than what one can imagine.'

'It sounds like we do have a challenge at hand, but what specifically do you want our help with?'

'Well, the agitation is becoming more organised and targeted by the day… They have started targeting specific corporate entities whose promoters are believed to be hand-in-glove with the current government. Over the past few days, several mobile towers belonging to one such company have been taken out in different districts. And such planning and execution requires funds… We need you to help us track these financiers.'

'That shouldn't be a problem. In fact, even the folks

at the ED should be able to do this in no time. All they need to do is to trace the money backwards to its source through the banking networks,' Ronit reasoned.

'If it were that simple, I wouldn't be here, would I?' Yadav, somewhat peeved, shot back. 'The money is being contributed by multiple individuals, NGOs and social bodies, and its destinations are also multiple. Either it is flowing in as contributions to the many farmer unions or these entities are spending it directly to fund specific initiatives. For instance, an NGO which was previously working towards providing education to underprivileged children has bought a dozen washing machines to support the agitation. They are installing these at the protest sites where farmers have congregated in large numbers, and they will be providing free laundry service to them… Imagine!'

Rohan concurred by pulling up his brows.

'The donors of this NGO include people from all walks of life, including some famous sportspersons and actors… Now, how on earth can we find any pattern in thousands of such random transactions, tell me?'

'There has to be a pattern… and let me see what we can do to identify it,' Ronit said.

'It's not going to be simple… The ED has already tried creating mock trails to trace these funds back to their sources but failed. Since we know that many of the suspect separatist organisations are running their operations from Canada, we even scrutinised all recent remittances from there. But once again, it yielded nothing,' Yadav explained.

'Well, the folks at the ED have their ways and we have ours. Let me get the team cracking on this immediately, and hopefully we will have something for you very soon,' Ronit said. He was looking at this as an opening to establish his department's worth in Yadav's eyes, and his mind was already scanning through the options available to them for initiating their probe. Yadav nodded and made a wordless exit.

Ronit leaned back on his chair, resting his head and craning his neck upwards in contemplation. This was when his hand involuntarily slipped inside his jacket pocket and his fingers brushed against something that wasn't supposed to be there—a neatly folded piece of paper. Puzzled, he pulled it out and spread it in front of him. It was a handwritten note:

> Mr Biswas,
>
> You don't know me, but you can consider me the friend that you need by your side right now.
>
> I have some information that you could use, and in return I want you to help me with some information as well—a simple and fair trade! And just to set the record straight, this is not a blackmail attempt or anything of that sort. This is just a proposed alliance between two people tied by commonality of purpose.
>
> I understand that you would look at this note with suspicion and apprehension; that is only natural, and I would have done so too. However, to put your doubts to rest, I am willing to share with you what I have

> purely in good faith. You can verify the veracity of the information and then decide whether you want to help me or not. No strings attached!
>
> If you are still thinking, think about this—what is there for you to lose? Absolutely nothing! And to make things convenient, I will meet you at the same coffee shop where you stop every morning, at say, 5.30 pm? Please be on time. A gentleman like you would know that it is rude to keep a lady waiting.
>
> —A Friend

Ronit remained staring at the note in bewilderment. This was classic cloak-and-dagger stuff that one might find in spy novels or movies, but not in his actual line of work. In his years at RAD, he had never even heard of any such happening from his colleagues.

Moreover, in the age of technology and science, who would go through all the trouble to slip a handwritten note in somebody's pocket? He could think of a hundred simpler and safer ways to send an anonymous message to someone. No one in his field of work would think of using such a primitive and precarious method. He was certain that someone was playing an amateurish prank on him, but he decided to give the note another read, nonetheless.

And then, a fleeting image appeared before his eyes. The image of a pretty girl dressed in an elegant Salwar Kameez who had accidently brushed past him outside Starbucks that morning. If someone had placed the note in his pocket, it had to be her. He went through the rest of the note, puzzled and curious, before another thought struck him. The note might not have anything to do with his professional life. The girl might be desirous of connecting with him in his personal capacity.

Ronit's suspicion that there was another man in his wife's life had been growing over the past months. It wasn't some incontrovertible evidence that he had uncovered, but a succession of small things that had been feeding his mistrust. Barkha's renewed affinity for her mobile phone, her instinctive reactions whenever he touched her and her sheer manner of talking (though they hadn't engaged much in talking lately) were all cues that he had been subconsciously registering.

He had been waiting for an opportunity, the right opportunity, to confront Barkha over his suspicions, but hadn't mustered the courage to do so yet. Perhaps it was his own guilt or maybe the absence of hard evidence that had been holding him back, but he knew that for the sake of his own peace it had to be done sooner than later.

'Maybe the time has come now,' Ronit thought. 'If there is another man in Barkha's life, the girl who had reached out to him could be his partner or spouse.' In light of this realisation, he read the note yet again, and everything appeared to fit in perfectly, like pieces of a simple jigsaw puzzle. This was the only plausible explanation, and if the note was anything to go by, the girl was going to give him the evidence he needed.

Ronit felt a shiver run down his spine at the thought.

Whether it was on account of anxiety, anticipation or pure apprehension, he couldn't tell.

He opened the bottom drawer of his desk and, after a bit of rummaging, retrieved a black colored pen from it. It was a standard issue spy camera with a micro camera built into its lid. It could record and store videos of up to one hour in duration. Ronit hadn't felt the need to use the device thus far, but he was glad that he had held on to it and not returned it to the supplies store. Today evening promised the perfect setting for the gadget to make a debut and prove its worth.

He checked the batteries, and once satisfied that they were still good, he relegated the pen to the top pocket of his jacket. After spending a few moments in adjusting the focus of the camera, Ronit shook his head vigorously, as though adjusting the focus of his thoughts now. He pulled a notepad and picked up a different pen to summarise his conversation with Yadav. Ronit wanted to make sure that he didn't miss out on any relevant pieces of information while briefing his team on the matter at hand.

Chapter 8

A Lot Happens Over Coffee

New Delhi, 23rd December 2020

The crisp breeze was adding to the nip of the evening air. The sun, or whatever demure version of it had shown up for the day, had already disappeared from the horizon by the time Ronit stepped out of the RAD complex. He had decided to walk to the coffee shop so as to avoid the pain of finding a parking spot, a decision he was already having second thoughts about.

He was walking briskly, shoulders hunched and hands in his pockets, with a bid to reduce his exposure to the chill. He wasn't much of a winter person, more so when he wasn't appropriately dressed for it.

As the flange with the green Starbucks logo became visible, Ronit reluctantly pulled out his left hand and glanced at the watch. It was 5.10 pm. He looked left and right before stepping inside.

The counter had a small queue of people waiting to

place their orders, but the seating area of the coffee shop was virtually empty. Ronit looked around and settled for a table adjacent to the window. From here he had a clear view of the street and could see his mysterious companion approach. Not that he was expecting her to spring any kind of surprise on him, but in his line of work he had witnessed caution saving lives in myriad normal seeming situations. It had become second nature to him now.

He waited for a few minutes, but it wasn't easy to sit idle with the inviting aroma of coffee tugging hard at him. And when he saw that the queue of customers had cleared, he couldn't resist getting up and making for the counter. It was rude not to wait for her before placing his order, but the walk in the cold had momentarily tweaked his worldview. He would have a second cup to keep her company, he told himself.

Ronit had been watching the door from the corner of his eye, and yet, as he turned around with his coffee, he found someone sitting across the chair he had been occupying moments ago. It was a dainty girl with large eyes and childlike features. She was looking straight back at him. At first Ronit was surprised at her sudden appearance, but when she blinked and curled her lips into a smile, he was quick to dismiss the incongruity. He smiled back and approached the table.

'Good evening, Mr Biswas,' she said rather formally, emerging from the chair and extending a hand.

'Hello,' Ronit said, shaking her hand. It was a surprisingly firm shake. 'I am sorry… I didn't know how long you were going to take, so I got this to keep me company,' he said, placing his cup on the table. 'What can I get for you?'

'A cappuccino please,' she returned with the same endearing smile.

Ronit adjusted the pen in his pocket as he waited for the barista to prepare her order, and when he returned to the table the camera was on and rolling.

'Here we go,' he said, placing the cup in front of her. 'I must say that I am bursting with curiosity though… It is not often that I am summoned for a coffee date by a mysterious young lady,' he added skittishly.

'I can imagine… Not surprising then that you want to record our meeting,' she said, pointing towards the pen with her eyes. The smile was still affixed on her face.

Ronit's condition was as if had been stung by a jellyfish. He tried to say something, but words seemed to be failing him.

'It's okay,' she said, coming to his rescue. She was unusually calm given the nature of the discovery she had just made. 'You don't know who I am or what I have called you here for… Had I been in your place, I would probably have done the same thing. I am fine with you recording the conversation… And to save you some time, let me get straight to the point.'

'I work at the embassy of a friendly country,' she said, pausing to check Ronit's reaction. He was still recovering from the earlier shock. 'You might want a name, and I could give you one, but we both know that it won't be correct. So, if it is okay with you, I will spare myself the trouble… Moreover, I am not here in my official capacity anyways, so it doesn't really matter…'

Ronit remained eyeing her incredulously. And when she paused, he finally murmured, 'What has Barkha done?'

'Barkha, who?' she returned, slightly surprised herself. 'Oh, of course… Barkha, your wife,' she recollected, and burst out laughing as soon as she made sense of what he was implying. 'No, no… I am not here to talk about Barkha. We can do that another day. For now, I am here to give you information on something far more overreaching and consequential… Not to say that Barkha is not consequential, but this pertains to a matter related to your nation's security.'

'I am listening,' Ronit said, unsure about his reactions to what he was hearing.

'Well, this is about the latest Chinese manoeuvre against India as part of the Operation Bamboo Garden,' she began. Then, sensing Ronit's discomfort, she added, 'You know about the Operation, don't you?'

'Yes… please continue. You were saying…,' Ronit hurriedly corrected his expressions. He had never come across the term *Operation Bamboo Garden*, unless it was the name of one of those Chinese food joints in Chanakyapuri. However, he had been taught to reveal less and listen more, especially under such circumstances.

'Okay, so, you might even know this, but the latest target of the Chinese Operation is the ongoing farmers' agitation here. In fact, I have evidence to prove that the Chinese are behind the escalation of these protests, and that they are doing so to further their larger nefarious objectives.'

Ronit was alarmed at the mention of the farmers' agitation. It was too much of a coincidence that the girl, whoever she was, had brought up the subject on the very same day that Yadav had sought his help on it. His mind was racing faster than a gazelle, thinking of ways to make her reveal more than her obviously practiced oratory.

He glanced around, suddenly aware that they were sitting in a coffee shop—not the most favourable setting for the kind of conversation this was turning into. He didn't notice anything or anyone suspicious.

Her eyes were affixed on him, studying even the slightest movement he made, and he thought he saw traces of a smile appear on her lips. It was the look of a confident shopkeeper allowing a potential customer to inspect her wares, certain that they would pass the test. In her silence, she seemed to be telling him that the venue was safe and that he was free to make his own assessments. Of course, it was Ronit's turn to respond, and she would wait for him to do so. The sparring match had begun and he was in too deep already. To bow out was no longer a viable option.

'You may be right, but why are you telling me all this? If indeed you are in possession of the sort of information you claim to have, you should approach one of the law enforcement agencies instead,' he interjected.

'As I said, I am not here to meet you in my professional

capacity,' she replied imperturbably, as if she had been expecting this argument. 'I am here because I need your help with something... Actually, allow me to paint a hypothetical picture here,' she said, flicking her eyes towards the pen in Ronit's pocket.

'So, let us assume that I am engaged in a vital mission for my country, which has me pitted against a common enemy of ours. This mission is so confidential that we can't formally approach your government for assistance. Let us say that it is something that doesn't involve India in any way, but my country cannot afford, for whatever it is, to come out in public...

'Now, something makes me realise that I might require the help of a specific person at some point in the future. Let's assume that the person is you... And during the course of my investigations, I also stumble upon some information that might not be relevant to me but could prove extremely valuable for you. Given this hypothetical background, would you not have approached me with the information, had our roles been reversed?'

'That's quite a story,' Ronit said mockingly. 'But let me narrate another hypothetical situation now. Suppose I get a mysterious note, from a woman I have never met, inviting me to join her for coffee. My curiosity gets the better of me and I oblige. During the coffee the woman, let's assume she is you, tells me that she is a foreign spy working on a mission, the details of which she can't share with me. She then seeks my help with God knows what, while refusing to share her name or even her nationality.

Now, had it been you in my place, would you have any good reason to trust the woman?'

'Now, that is a smart way to put it,' she replied, maintaining her smile. 'And to tell you the truth, I would find it very hard—almost impossible, actually—to believe her… However, your hypothesis is based on a couple of assumptions. First, that the woman wants you to trust her, and second, she is seeking your help. If both these assumptions turn out to be false, you have no reason to be wary of her.'

'Okay, now you have me thoroughly confused.'

'Ha, ha, ha,' she chuckled. 'Yes, all this hypothesising is just too much, isn't it? Okay, let me try and simplify it for you… I am not seeking any help from you. As I said, I might need your help in the future, and then again, I might not. For now, I am here only to share the information I have uncovered. You can have it verified through your own sources and then decide if you want to act on it. I have a feeling, though, that had you known what this information is, you would have given an arm and a leg to get your hands on it.'

'And this information, what if I take it right now and decline to help you later?'

'The information I am giving you is not conditional. Whether or not you find it useful, you can choose if you want to help me based on the merit of my request. That too if we ever come to it... Now, Mr Biswas, I doubt if you would have ever come across a sweeter deal than this,' she said playfully.

Ronit had been conditioned to believe that anything which appeared too good to be true had to have a hidden, crooked side to it. The deal that the girl was offering was no different. However, despite his best efforts, he couldn't think of how he could possibly be exposing himself by accepting the information that she was so intent on giving him. Of course, a part of Ronit wanted him to trust the girl. She was so delicate, so innocent looking, that he couldn't picture her as someone even having a deceitful and devious shade to her. This part of him was drawing Ronit against his own instincts, but he was too absorbed in the conversation to take note.

'As I mull over the terms of this supposedly once-in-a-lifetime deal, would you want to at least tell me what specifically is this evidence that you have unearthed?'

'You are an impatient man, aren't you, Mr Biswas? Well, what I have for you is this,' she said, placing her palm on the table and leaving behind a small pen drive as she pulled it back. 'This contains transaction trails to prove how Chinese money is being routed to certain sections of the agitators using the network of communist organisations and sympathisers in your country. This might not cover all the channels that they have activated to funnel the money, but it will certainly account for a major portion of it. And be prepared to be shocked by their ingenious ways. The transactions are so cleverly disguised that they would seamlessly pass through any scrutiny by your financial watchdogs. It was only by chance that they caught my eye.'

'It is very modest of you to say so,' Ronit interjected sarcastically. The gravity of the situation notwithstanding, he was enjoying the silly banter with the girl whose name he didn't know. It was quite ironic, but in a long time he had not felt so comfortable and at ease in the company of a woman.

'You don't believe me?' she returned in a put-on angry tone. 'Okay, tell me… The last Bollywood blockbuster which grossed over five hundred crore rupees globally, what percentage of it came from China? Let me tell you—over twenty percent of the movie's collections were from the Chinese Mainland! In value terms, this is equal or slightly more than the collections of a somewhat successful medium-budget Chinese film. Have you ever thought how these dubbed Hindi movies are doing so much business in a country where most theatres are found screening locally made movies?'

'You mean the distribution proceeds of these movies are deliberately inflated by the Chinese to plough money into our country?' Ronit shot out, surprised.

'Exactly! And here you will see how it is only a handful of exhibitors and distributors whose films seem to be receiving disproportionate love from Chinese cinegoers. You will also see how the same individuals are linked to a common set of social causes in one or the other manner, including the farmers' agitation. And guess what, each one of them has contributed money to a farmer union or an NGO working with these protesters.'

'Wow,' was all Ronit could say.

'This is just the tip, my dear, the iceberg is in here,' she said, pointing at the storage device. 'Go, have your experts work on it and you will be able to corroborate every single transaction that is mentioned here. All the best,' she said, getting up from her chair.

'You are leaving? But what if... what if I need to contact you about something? How can I get in touch with you?'

'Don't worry, I will find you,' she said, sporting her trademark smile. Then, she turned on her heels and strode out of the coffee shop. It was only after another fifteen minutes that Ronit could muster the courage to get up from his seat. The mysterious girl had left him jolted in more ways than one.

Chapter 9

Decoding Bamboo Garden

New Delhi, 28th December 2020

'We think we might have something for you on the farmers' protest, but before I invite the team to brief us, I want you to tell me everything you know about Operation Bamboo Garden,' Ronit said, as soon as Yadav had plunged himself on a chair. Ronit had fixed the update meeting with Yadav and his team and had requested for some time alone with the veteran before others joined in. They were presently seated in one of the RAD meeting rooms.

'Bamboo Garden? What does that have to do with the farmers' agitation?' Yadav responded. But Ronit's stern look forced him to change gears. 'Well, if you must know… it is a term coined by some journalist for the Chinese policy of economic annexation. You know, how they give infrastructure loans to smaller countries at exorbitant rates and when the recipients are unable to service the loans, the Chinese grab their land or arm-twist them into making severe commercial concessions. But again, why have you suddenly developed interest in all this?'

'Do you have any indications to suggest that they might be looking to increase their influence in the Indian economy as well?' Ronit continued, without bothering to respond to Yadav's question.

'China certainly looks at India as a threat to its domination in the region, and the two countries haven't been on the best of terms since 1962. Every now and then, the Chinese try to ruffle us through undue aggression on the northern borders or through unsavoury diplomatic actions. You know that they have been using their veto power to block our membership to the UN Security Council for the past several years, just like they have sided with Pakistan and snowballed all our efforts to hold them accountable for harbouring and abetting known terrorists. But to say that they might have included India as a target for Operation Bamboo Garden and might be trying to gain control of our economy is farfetched. Our economy is based on sound fundamentals, and I don't believe that the Chinese will get anywhere with us even if they decide to get adventurous.'

'Your patriotism, Mr Yadav, is beyond doubt, but I am afraid it might not be enough to stop the Chinese from doing what they intend to do. You know how they have gradually increased their influence in the US economy, and now they account for nearly five percent of the US federal government debt… Not to forget how several European nations have accused the Chinese of spreading the coronavirus just so they could cheaply buy out stakes in global corporations operating on their soil. The claims regarding the virus might or might not be true, but we all know how Chinese corporations have benefitted from the pandemic across the globe. So, if they are not weary of taking on the Western superpowers, I suspect that the so-called strong fundamentals of our economy will prove much of a deterrent for them… I think we should analyse the situation dispassionately before arriving at any conclusions.'

The pen drive that the mysterious woman had handed over to Ronit had turned out to be a treasure trove of information. It had details of hundreds of monetary transactions originating in China or from Chinese entities elsewhere, and after passing through a complex web of transmissions they were finding their way into India. The Indian recipients included 47 individuals and organisations whose names were in some way of the other associated with the ongoing farmers' agitation.

Ronit and his team had worked over the past three days to validate the financial information and to dive deep into the cyber presence of each of these 47 names. They had scanned websites, tracked their activities and contacts on social media and even hacked emails in some cases to gather all relevant details and evidence that they could. 'As far as we can help, none of these offenders should walk away for want of evidence. Let us not leave any stone unturned. It is up to us to bring these enemies of our nation to justice,' Ronit had repeatedly reminded his team through the course of the investigation.

In the end, the story that emerged was distressing and frightful to say the least. The tidbits of information they had gathered—random chats, posts and emails containing specific keywords—did not reveal much in isolation; but when pieced together, they painted an ominous picture. The details suggested that instigating the farmers was part of a much larger Chinese plot against India, and the seeds of this conspiracy had been sown much before the Farm Bills were even drafted. The term *Operation Bamboo Garden* had also appeared in some of the transcripts.

Everyone in the room was left horror-stricken at the discovery. However, despite their best efforts, they could not come up with any concrete pointers on what the larger conspiracy might be. It was soon clear that they were up against a vigilant adversary, and that the full contours of the scheme were probably known only to a handful of people in Beijing who were certainly not discussing it on social media.

The team had even backtracked the contacts of the Indian connivers up to several degrees to arrive at a set of Chinese names who were apparently holding the threads of the conspiracy. But that is where the trail ran cold. The cyber sleuths could not proceed beyond this list, no matter how hard they tried, leading them to the conclusion that these names were either fictitious or of merely bit players who were acting on the instructions of a far more powerful and sinister enemy—the secret police agency of the People's Republic of China, better known as the Ministry of State Security.

This was when Ronit took the decision to read Yadav in. The gravity of the situation demanded that they put their heads together against the common enemy. Instructing Myra to collate their findings, he had called Yadav's office to set up a meeting at the earliest possible.

'What do you suppose the Chinese are up to this time?' Yadav asked after a momentary pause. The fact that he had not countered Ronit's argument was an indication that he saw some truth in it.

'Let me call the team to brief us on what they have figured out,' he replied, stepping forward to open the door. Ronit took two steps and returned right back in. On his heels were Adhiraj and Myra. A few steps behind them was Jason, an officer from the International Affairs desk that Yadav had summoned by a wave of his hand. They took up the empty chairs after greeting the superiors.

'Myra, why don't we get started right away,' Ronit suggested.

'Sure,' she returned, plugging the projector chord into her laptop.

After setting a brief context, she began, 'Chinese misadventures are nothing new to India. Be it the military buildup along our shared borders or their claim of Arunachal Pradesh being an integral part of China, they have never shied away from provoking us. However, for the sake of this discussion, I will restrict myself to a series of recent events which, by the rapid succession of their occurrence, appear to be connected.'

'The most devastating Chinese gift to the world has been the coronavirus. We know about its calamitous impact on humanity, but the Covid-19 pandemic also sent most global economies into a tailspin, including ours,' Myra continued, using the clicker to bring up relevant images and statistics on the screen. 'Our economy had barely started to emerge from the impact of the lockdown when the military confrontation in Ladakh happened. Not only did many of our brave soldiers lose their lives, but we were forced to equip our troops for retaining their positions through the harsh winter months. The investments required in equipment and armaments ran into millions of dollars and this unplanned expenditure further aggravated our budgetary deficits.'

'How is all this related to the protesting farmers?' Yadav interjected impatiently.

'I am getting to that, Sir… Agriculture is the primary source of livelihood for fifty-eight percent of our population. Imagine, if more than half our population were to come up in arms against the government and engage in vandalism and destruction of public property, what could it lead to? The protests, which were largely peaceful so far, have already started shifting gears. We know that mobile towers belonging to one specific service provider have been vandalised in several places, leading to a sharp drop in the company's share prices. Lakhs of Indians who have invested their life's savings in this company have lost all their money…'

Myra went on to explain how multiple monetary trails indicated that the sustenance and escalation of the protests were being ensured using Chinese money. Yadav was listening intently, and he didn't quiz her on how they had identified the transactions that had escaped even the ED's radar. Had the question come up, Myra would have been unable to answer it. Ronit had kept the source of this explosive information concealed from everyone, including his team.

'This is some fantastic work you guys have done,' Yadav remarked, first looking at Myra and then shifting his gaze towards Ronit. 'The tragedy is that despite knowing what these traitors are up to, we won't be able to lay a finger on them.' The disappointment in his voice was apparent as he eyed the names of the Indian co-conspirators flashing on the screen.

'But why, Sir? We have the details right down to the transaction ids. The information can be validated by their banks. This is concrete evidence…,' Myra shot out surprised.

'This is evidence, alright, but circumstantial at best. The transactions have all been declared and purportedly the money has exchanged hands on legitimate grounds. Now, whether a Bollywood movie did the claimed amount of business, or a cricketer was indeed paid such a hefty endorsement fee by a Chinese company, are questions that only the Chinese can answer. And I doubt if the Chinese would willingly send anyone to testify in Indian courts against their own stooges… This too will matter only if we are able to arrest and charge any of these people. With the wave of sympathy that the farmers are garnering across the globe, the minute we apprehend anyone, we will have the whole world screaming foul. Activists and human rights groups will proclaim it to be an act of vendetta, and the government will become an even bigger villain than it is currently being made out to be.'

'But don't worry,' Yadav continued, after pausing briefly to look at Myra's drooping face, 'what you have uncovered is worth its weight in gold. We have our own ways of keeping these anti-national elements in check. And now that we know who is orchestrating all this, we will alert the appropriate agencies and they will know what to look for. We might not be able to reverse the damage, but this information will help us contain it for sure.'

He looked at Ronit and said, 'Thank you,' before leaving his chair.

As he watched Yadav and Jason exit the room, Ronit's lips curved into a smirk. This was the first time that the RAD veteran had expressed gratitude towards something that his department had done. Coming from him, the appreciation meant the world to the head of the Department of Cybercrime. To Ronit, this was a sign that his department was finally coming into its own.

And then, without a warning, his thoughts darted back at the mysterious girl who had made it all possible. By now, Ronit was grinning ear to ear, much to Adhiraj and Myra's amusement. He felt a strong urge to meet her and to thank her in person. Just when he was about to pull out his mobile phone to call her, he realised that she had not given him her number. He could do nothing but to wait for her to establish contact.

'Good job done, you both! And now let us keep going… Let's see if we can unravel anything more on this Operation Bamboo Garden,' he said to Myra and Adhiraj, before going on to give them a summary of what he had learnt about the Operation from Yadav. Work was a tried and tested antidote for the helplessness and despair that was threatening to drown Ronit on the personal front. The mystery girl had been on his mind ever since he had met her. And now, when he had good reason to contact her, his inability to do so was vexing him to no end.

Chapter 10

The Tumult Within

New Delhi, 5th January 2021

The new year had been ushered in with much hope and anticipation across the globe, albeit in a relatively subdued avatar. 2021 was being touted as a year of resurgence and ascent by all of humanity. The worst of the pandemic was over, or at least that is what most believed, and several vaccines were in advance stages of trial or awaiting emergency usage approvals. Humankind was once again going to prevail, and things were going to return to normal. Or were they?

In Ronit's small world, not much had changed with the turn of the calendar. The only noteworthy progress he had made was a name—Anmol. More than once, when Barkha's phone had vibrated with an incoming message, he had seen this name flash on the locked screen. The giveaway, though, was the coy smile that spontaneously appeared whenever she read these messages.

'Who is this Anmol? Never heard of him earlier,' he had managed to ask her one time. The seemingly innocuous question had taken all his grit and enough mental rehearsals before it could be voiced.

He thought he saw her face changing shades, but she was quick to recover. 'He's Meetu's brother-in-law… We had met when I was visiting her once. Nice guy!' she responded.

Even before he could come up with a follow-up question, she added, 'I am going to make some tea. You want some?' And that was the end of the conversation. The chance to confront her that Ronit had so painstakingly created had been flung out of the window just like that.

Another time and this setback would have forced Ronit to put his curiosity at bay for the time being, but not now. Something within him had changed ever since he had met the mystery girl. No, he wasn't in love. He couldn't be. Even though the mystery girl had an innate attractive quality to her, Ronit was in love with the woman he had tied the nuptial knot with. Still.

It was perhaps the baggage of his unfulfilled expectations that was troubling him. When he had received the cryptic message, he had convinced himself that the stranger was going to provide him proof of Barkha's infidelity. The thought had infuriated him, but he had braced himself for what he believed was coming his way.

It wasn't easy. The thought that Barkha's affections might have found a different beneficiary was harsh.

It brought with it a distinct discomfort in his belly, as though his innards were being grated, but he continued to entertain it, nevertheless. Ronit, it seemed, was marinating his mind, prepping it to bear the disclosure that he was expecting to be made that evening.

And when his meeting with the mysterious girl returned a contrary outcome, he was left to contend with the burden of curiosity he had called upon himself. Each time he thought about the mystery woman— something he had been doing at an alarming frequency—he would end up thinking about the man that Barkha was cheating on him with. Instantly he would feel the burden return to weigh him down.

It might have been the urgent need to solve this puzzle that had lent him the courage to ask Barkha about Anmol in the first place. The confrontation had been avoided and Barkha had refused to take the bait, but that had done little to settle his unrest. The turmoil within his head had remained brewing.

Ronit was sitting on the couch, pensively eyeing Barkha's mobile phone. The phone was connected to a charging socket near the TV trolley.

After he had returned from office, Barkha had served him his customary evening tea and then announced that she was stepping out to buy groceries. Since her phone was low on battery, she had opted against carrying it with her.

At the sight of her unattended phone, a sudden thought inadvertently sprung in his head. The thought was repulsive, at least by the high standards that Ronit set for himself, and he tried to brush it aside. But it persisted, forcing him to acknowledge its existence. The thought persisted, darting from one corner of his brain to another, losing its sting with each passing moment. In his head it was gradually drifting from the domain to inappropriateness to an action he could actually consider.

'This is the only way for you to know what she's hiding. If she is indeed cheating on you, you will be committing a much lesser transgression in comparison. Think about your own peace of mind...,' he could hear a familiar voice yelling inside his head. This was nothing but Ronit's unconfessed yearning prodding him, and there was no countering its justifications and reasoning.

He glanced at the wall clock and his decision was firmed up instantly. It was already ten minutes since Barkha had left and, if she decided to skip the vegetable hawker on her way back from the store, she would be home in another fifteen to twenty minutes.

'Fuck it,' he said out aloud, getting up from the couch to extract his laptop from the office bag. He pulled the chord that connected Barkha's phone to the charger and plugged it to his laptop instead. For the next few minutes Ronit furiously played with the laptop keys, alternatively watching the door and the clock with the corner of his eyes. When he stopped, he stared at the laptop screen until a victorious smile replaced the frown on his face. It took him little time to return the gadgets to their original positions, and he was back on the couch, fiddling with the TV remote once again.

Breaching the phone's much-touted security was child's play for the head of RAD's Department of Cybercrime. He could do this in his sleep. Barkha's phone had been duly cloned and a copy of it rested in Ronit's hard drive now. All he needed to do was click on an icon on his laptop and he would have access to all her chats, including her message exchanges with Anmol. As long as the laptop was connected to the internet, he could even eavesdrop on her telephonic conversations whenever he wanted.

Ronit was staring at the TV screen, basking in his small victory, and waiting for his wife to return with the groceries when his own phone chimed. It was a message from a masked number that read: 'Mr Biswas, it is a little rude to not respond to a greeting. Don't you think?'

He scrolled up and found a simple 'Happy New Year' message in the chat history.

Ronit wasn't a big fan of exchanging greetings over text messages. He felt that the medium had eroded the human touch and genuine expression of sentiments that such occasions demanded. Be it the New Year, Independence Day or one of the many festivals, he found his chats flooded with greetings, a majority of them from people he could barely place. Although he made it a point to respond to the messages from his acquaintances, he summarily ignored the ones sent from unfamiliar numbers. Of course, he never initiated an exchange of such greetings with anyone. He preferred calling and speaking to those he genuinely felt like wishing.

'Undisclosed Number,' was all that his phone revealed

of the sender's identity. It was a common practice for people in his line of work to keep their contact details masked and the greeting had been too commonplace for him to pay any heed. But the recent message was different. The tonality and play of words seemed to suggest that the sender was someone he had been eagerly waiting to hear from.

He typed a reply, read it, and being not entirely satisfied, deleted it. It was only in his third attempt that the words on the screen managed to pass his scrutiny. Ronit wasn't entirely pleased with them, but he decided to send it anyway. There was a limit to how impressively he could compose a sentence with seven words. The message read: *Is this who I think it is?*

'That depends on who you are thinking about ;)' came a prompt reply.

Ronit didn't know many people who spoke with him in this manner. Something told him that the sender was the mystery girl, the very girl who had been springing up in his thoughts like wildflowers in an unkempt garden ever since he had met her. But he couldn't chance a guess over a text message. What if it turned out to be a prank by someone known to Barkha?

He was still eyeing the phone screen pensively, typing and deleting random letters, when another message alert sounded. 'It's about time we meet again, don't you think?'

'Of course, let me know when and where,' he replied with considerable confidence now.

'Don't worry about that. I will find you at a good time :)'

The conversation was brief, but it was sufficient to draw Ronit from his worldly worries into a world of anxious anticipation. He could feel the eagerness and enthusiasm of a teenager heading out for his first date.

Barkha returned with the groceries soon thereafter, and after a few perfunctory exchanges, made for the kitchen. Her words had barely registered with Ronit though. The unexpected exchange of messages had transported him into an entirely different realm, where Barkha or the clone of her phone resting on his laptop didn't seem to matter. The mystery girl, he thought, was like an illicit drug pulling him into her orbit. And he found himself blindly complying, unable and unwilling to resist.

Chapter 11

A Lustful Encounter

Gurugram, 5th January 2021

The Sector-29 market in Gurugram is the Jekyll and Hyde equivalent of bazaars.

During the daytime, establishments serving pizza, burgers and traditional Indian fare attract food connoisseurs and families from across the city and beyond. Hawkers can be seen selling balloons, colourful toys, handicrafts and other such items in the open parking space encircled by the string of eateries. Children dragging their parents, cajoling them for a ride on the radiantly embellished camels or to get them a toy is a common sight. In short, it is the perfect destination for a happy family outing with something on offer for everyone.

It is with the setting sun that the Sector-29 market begins to transform. As the numerous bars and pubs, many of them located on the floors above the family establishments, start coming to life, the market dons an entirely different look. Bright neon signs, cacophony of pulsating music and groups of youngsters—many shy of even the legal drinking age, turn the market into a vivacious and happening nightspot. The children and families, after a day of fun and frolic, recede to their homes, vacating the spot for raucous partygoers and merrymakers.

Sector-29 was the first nightspot to come up in the city, and it catered to revellers from all walks of life, including the corporate gentry of Gurugram, until other plush hotspots emerged and drew away the moneyed and genteel. Heightened competition among existing joints led to a price war of sorts, and in time, Sector-29 found its niche as the pocket-friendly party place of Gurugram. Students, entry level corporate executives and smaller businessmen who sought to let their hair down without denting their finances considerably now constituted the usual clientele for the bars and pubs in the area. If rumours were to be believed, the market was fast becoming an epicentre for drugs and the flesh trade, further dissuading polite society from visiting the area post nightfall.

It was shortly after 9 pm that a rickety Maruti Zen swerved inside the open parking lot of the Sector-29 market. The driver was a rotund man who stepped out of the vehicle with some difficulty. The car model, which even the manufacturers had pulled out of the market by now, didn't quite offer the headroom that his massive frame demanded.

Keeping the car door ajar, he extracted a pocket comb

from the glove compartment and brushed his hair. He then used his palms to straighten the creases on his pink polo tee, which had been neatly tucked inside his loose-fitting denims. The t-shirt was already stretched under considerable pressure from his protruding belly, and it was nothing short of a miracle that he found some wrinkles that still needed straightening. He then eyed himself from top to bottom, and satisfied, slammed the car door before striding towards one of the bars.

It was not long since the sun had exited the horizon, and the place was virtually empty. He looked around and settled for a small table on the far side of the bar counter. He had barely deposited himself on the chair when a waiter swooped in and thrust a menu card in his hand. The man studied the listings before pointing to a familiar brand of bottled beer. The joint boasted of an in-house microbrewery that produced six different varieties of ale and its regular patrons preferred these to the bottled ones. This guest clearly wasn't a regular patron and neither did he appear to be a beer connoisseur. The waiter scribbled the order mechanically and made a quiet exit.

The man, after a quick visual survey of his surroundings pulled out his mobile phone and swiped it to life. He glanced at the screen before clicking on an icon that resembled the silhouette of a burning flame. As he clicked on the latest trail of message exchanges his lips curled into a half smile.

It was only last evening that the dating app had notified him of a match. The girl in the pictures was striking, but he had stopped his expectations from soaring. He had been on the platform long enough to know that a sizeable number of people used pictures downloaded from the internet to keep their real identities under wraps. While the pictures on his own profile were real, even he was using a pseudonym and a generously pruned declaration of his age. There was no reason to believe that the profile he had matched with was a real one.

To test the waters, he sent her a message. It was a perfunctory greeting, and he received a courteous response within the minute. He replied with a few basic questions and once again the revert was quick. The girl, he learnt, was originally from Nepal and she was pursuing her master's degree course in Delhi. The introduction, her pictures and her response time were all pointing towards something promising, but once again he had to control his excitement and eagerness.

If she was indeed who she proclaimed to be, why would she choose to connect with someone like him? Despite his reduced displayed age, she was considerably younger, and he harboured no misconceptions about his looks either. She could have found hundreds of younger and better-looking men to match with on the dating app. Why him then?

He had heard stories and read articles about young girls using dating applications to solicit men with the purpose of making some additional pocket money. 'Sugar daddy': He recalled this is how an article had referred to the older men who got into *quid pro quo* arrangements with these girls.

He wasn't averse to the idea of paying money if it satisfied his carnal desires, especially with a partner as stunning as her, but his middleclass financial prudence had prevented him from exploring this avenue thus far. His aversion, he knew, was at best a spot of grey and he was not strictly against stretching his boundaries if the right opportunity came by. The position of money in his life was no more than a matter of his own convenience. When it came to the *unreasonable* demands of his wife—spending on new bedlinen or gifts for a relative they were visiting—it became a scarce and precious commodity, while for his own desires it was simply a means of fulfilling them. So, as he remained exchanging messages with her, a part of him wished that she would propose a mutually beneficial arrangement of some sort.

She didn't.

Instead, she remained chit-chatting, unabashedly sharing her own story with him. Her roommate had left for her hometown days before the lockdown was announced, leaving her to endure the following months of solitary confinement. It had been a harrowing experience, expectedly, and with the ground situation improving, she was itching to step out and have some fun. Her plight, and more so, the fact that she had decided to confide in him with it carried a promise that was hard to ignore. He could feel something warm and fuzzy welling up in his belly.

He remained chatting with her till the wee hours, indifferent to the petite frame lying beside him on the bed, emitting soft snores intermittently. By the time he put the phone to rest he had arranged to meet the girl the next evening, and that, without any financial considerations. He went to bed smiling, feeling smug about what he had managed to achieve.

The next evening, he had returned from work early and changed into something he thought was appropriate for the occasion. His son, the only occupant of the house who enjoyed enough liberty to be able to quiz him on his plans, was out for his tuitions, sparing the need to lie. 'I will be late, don't wait for me,' was all he proffered to his wife, as he stepped out of the house. She responded with a meek nod.

It was nearly ten minutes after the designated time that she stepped inside the bar. He spotted her instantly. For the past ten minutes his eyes had been affixed on the entrance, blinking only when necessary, as his mind painted grim images of what might transpire. It wasn't unusual for people, men especially, to get stood up on such blind dates. It wasn't a thought he was willingly entertaining, but he was unable to wish it away either.

Thus, he felt a wave of relief gush through him upon her sight, and he waved ferociously to catch her eye.

She smiled, waved back and made for his table. She sashayed like a model on a ramp and her slender and toned body only helped bolster this analogy. She was wearing a black denim skirt and boots, topped with a loose-fitting sweater. She was glamorous and exotic, and he half expected her to take a good look at him and make a hasty retreat. But she didn't.

'Hello,' she said, extending a hand as she deposited herself on the empty chair across him. Her trained grip was like a naked electric wire, and he suddenly felt several amperes of current running through his body. 'You started already?' she added, drawing her brows to glance at his empty pint. He could only muster a smile.

The girl—she claimed the name on the app was her real one, Sonam—appeared unfazed by his looks or by the obvious difference in their age. She seemed genuinely happy to have found another human being to talk to. By his third pint and her second glass of wine, his inhibitions had all but evaporated and the two were chatting like they had known each other forever. Of course, as he grew in comfort, his longing for her continued to rise steadily.

'This is so much fun,' she said merrily.

'What?' he was forced to scream at the top of his voice. The music too, like his desires, had stepped up, making it difficult for them to hear each other. By now he had lost count of the number of pints he had guzzled, and her words were sounding thick and lazy too.

'This is so much fun… I wish I didn't have to go back,' she shouted back.

'Then don't go,' he returned spontaneously, looking straight into her eyes. She held his gaze for a moment. The pause was enough for his alcohol induced courage to wane. He instantly diverted his attention towards his beer, bracing for invectives that were bound to be showered upon him. But what he heard next surprised him to no end.

'But where can we go? I am sure we can't head to your place; your family will be around…,' she said, purposely letting her words tail.

The opportunity was too good to pass. 'I know a good and safe hotel nearby… I am too drunk to drive back, and I was planning to stay there for the night anyway. If you want, you can join me,' he offered.

He was glad to have suggested the Sector 29 market as the venue for their meeting. Since last evening, when the plan had been finalised, he had been experiencing an unusual rush of testosterone. Although the chat had carried no sexual innuendos, he couldn't let go of the hormone-induced hope and the idea that anything was possible after a few rounds of drinks. He had heard about inexpensive and discreet hotels near the market that could prove useful if the need did emerge.

It was this optimism that had given him the courage to drive all the way to Gurugram to meet her. Of course, there was the need to keep his nefarious dalliances distanced from home or any nearby areas where he might run into an acquaintance, but that was more of an afterthought. He had taken a punt and it was about to yield rich dividends.

He would need no more than a few minutes on his phone to find a hotel that valued customers' money more than the absurd regulations around ascertaining and recording their identities. He was far away from his home in Central Delhi, and that left him with precious little to worry about. He could enter and leave the hotel accompanied by the lovely young girl without the risk of being spotted or recognised.

'Are you sure that won't be a problem?' she said, attempting to add a touch of apprehension to a decision that had already been sealed.

'Of course, I am sure… Let me call for the bill,' he said excitedly.

His heart was galloping like a highbred horse on steroids. He was beaming, like a man who had made an impossible wish, only to find that it had been granted. The heaven he had dreamt of was soon going to become a reality, and he was already picturing himself lying blissfully in the lap of the celestial angel accompanying him.

Chapter 12

Another Cup Of Coffee

New Delhi, 6th January 2021

It was a windy morning, and Ronit found solace in the cozy confines of his car as he slipped inside after the brief but excruciating walk in the cold. Having pulled the door shut, he was blowing on his fingers, readying them for the drive ahead, when a knock on the passenger side window startled him. The intruder was a woman, he could gather, but she was standing upright, making it impossible for him to see her face or ascertain her identify.

'Hi… Do I know you?' he asked curiously, rolling down a few inches of the glass and craning his neck. He hadn't noticed another human form in the vicinity while stepping inside the vehicle. It was eerie how the woman had suddenly appeared by the car to knock on the glass. *Who was the woman, and where had she suddenly surfaced from? Why was she trying to draw his attention?*

She made no efforts to bend or step back, keeping

him deprived of a glance to aid recognition. After a brief pause, she said, 'You know me well enough, Mr Biswas… And if you don't mind, can I get inside? It is pretty cold out here, you know.'

Ronit's heart skipped a beat instantly. The mischievous, accented voice was unmistakable. It was the same voice that had been ringing in his ears at the oddest hours over the past few days. The voice belonged to the mysterious girl who had remained in his thoughts ever since they had first met. He reached out, disengaged the lock and pushed the door open.

'Good morning,' she said, getting inside.

Ronit returned the greeting, trying hard to maintain a straight face. The message exchanges from last evening had left him optimistic and even upbeat about meeting her again, but he wasn't expecting the encounter to happen so soon. A part of him was thrilled to see her, and yet he couldn't help but feel a sense of alarm at the sudden encounter. The apprehension was perhaps on account of his knowledge about her profession. Given the circumstances, he thought it best to keep his reactions concealed.

'You don't seem particularly excited to see me?'

'Excited, I wouldn't know, but surprised I certainly am,' he returned, engaging the gears to back up the vehicle. 'I assume you are heading in the same direction as I am?'

'I thought I told you last evening that I will find you at a good time, and this is as good a time as any… isn't it?

Though, after the information I gave you, I was hoping for an expression of gratitude of some sort. A smile perhaps?' she persisted in her unique coquettish manner.

Ronit suddenly felt nervous and shaky. He was finding it hard to focus on the road ahead. 'And why would you assume that the information was any good?' he said, mostly on account of his own inability to come up with a better response.

She burst out laughing in response, and then she added, 'Really? We are going to start playing this cat and mouse game now? If the information was useless, how come your Narcotics Control Bureau has opened investigations on several celebrities and influential citizens? It must be a mere coincidence that most of these names find a mention in the list that I gave you, right?'

Ronit was taken aback. The information she had given him was airtight, alright, but he wasn't aware of any action that Yadav had initiated against the names on the list. And if he had, Ronit had not been kept in the loop. The girl was certainly better informed than him, and he opted to shield himself with silence to prevent his impuissance from showing.

'What I provided you was information and not concrete evidence. It couldn't help you bring these people to book, but it had to have passed your tests of authenticity for you to deploy alternate methods to contain them… Tell me that my assessment is incorrect!'

He could sense that she was staring right at him as she spoke. So, avoiding her gaze, he said, 'And I bet you haven't turned suddenly to extract an acknowledgement of the authenticity of your information from me.' This was a textbook technique to skirt uncomfortable questions and steer a conversation in the direction one desired. Ronit was happy to have recalled the technique at the right instance and having deployed it effectively.

'You are right,' she said, her words acquiring a more consequential tone. 'There is something else that has brought me to you… But can we stop somewhere, perhaps for a cup of coffee, so that I have your undivided attention when we talk?'

'I usually don't go on coffee dates with strangers… Yes, exceptions have been made in the past, but not beyond the first meeting. A second coffee date would at least warrant a name,' he said, glancing at her from the corner of his eye. It was his turn to switch on his charm now.

She laughed a tinkling little laugh and said, 'Makes sense… Hi, I am Noor!'

'Glad to meet you, Noor. I am Ronit,' he returned, turning to look at her as they broke into simultaneous smiles.

Shortly after, Ronit's car was swerving inside the gated entrance of The Claridges Hotel. The thought of heading to his usual coffee shop, the one where they had first met, did occur to him, but he was quick to drop the idea. It was too close to his place of work and the setting hardly offered the privacy that a conversation with the mystery girl warranted. Of course, a subconscious attempt to impress Noor with his choice of an upscale venue wouldn't have been an entirely inaccurate guess either.

As they were led to their table in the hotel coffee shop, Ronit struggled to take his eyes off her. He had deliberately fallen a step behind to keep her in his natural line of vision. She wore a grey business suit with a button-up shirt, and walked on the balls of her feet, fizzing with infectious energy. Seated across him, she could easily pass for an investment advisor guiding him on ways to make his millions count. The trouble was that he was yet to save his millions.

They waited patiently until the maître d had receded after recording their coffee orders. Ronit had used this time to text Adhiraj and inform him that he would be reaching office late.

'So then, what is this all about?' he finally said, breaking the silence. The coffee shop appeared understaffed, as did the hotel, but quite enough hands to service the few customers around. The venue was quite a progress from the one where she had invited him last time around.

'I want your help to track someone ... A dangerous Chinese operative, who we call Zhiming. We have reasons to believe that she is operating in your country for the past several months.'

'Just like that?' he said once he had assimilated the ask. 'I mean, you just turn up one fine day, tell me that a foreign spy is functioning on our soil and expect me to jump on the prospects of helping you track her down. Do you really think this is all so simple?'

It was here, the time to deliver against the information that she had given him, and his guard was up. He didn't know what shenanigans this innocent looking girl was trying to weave, but he wasn't going to let her play him. She had offered the information. He hadn't asked for it. And he had not committed to doing anything for her in return. He would not allow her to manipulate him and take on any task that he felt even a wee bit uncomfortable about.

'It is not simple by any stretch of the imagination... Like we had agreed, whether you help me or not is solely your decision. I only intend to share some facts and present a case to help you make up your mind. So, if you will please bear with me,' she said, reaching out for something inside her handbag. She extracted a bundle of printed sheets and sifted through them before handing him one.

'Do you recognise this man?' It was a copy of a newspaper clipping, announcing the untimely death of a Taiwanese businessman.

'This is Reng Fei, the founder of one of the largest chip manufacturing companies in the world, a Taiwanese national. He was a noted philanthropist, space enthusiast and, to his peril, a vociferous supporter of the Taiwanese freedom movement. He had received awards from several world bodies and had even broken into the list of the wealthiest men in the world a few years back. That was the time he felt he could use his global stature to further the cause of his country's freedom. He gave interviews to international media outlets, where he exposed Chinese control of his country's media, their meddling in Taiwan's elections and even the attempts to undermine their economic independence. He appealed to world leaders, many dependent on the chips his company produced, to further Taiwan's digital agenda and bolster the country's financial standing. And that is how he ended up painting a target on his back.'

Ronit had stopped reading the paper and was intently listening to her now. The article was no more than a factual account of how the lifeless body of the entrepreneur was discovered inside his penthouse in Taipei. The cause of death, the article revealed, was sudden cardiac arrest and the authorities had ruled out any kind of foul play.

'A few weeks before his death, the proprietary manufacturing technology of his company was leaked to his competitors. It was claimed that this was the doing of a mischievous hacker. Consequently, his company's stocks plummeted across all major exchanges and almost his entire net worth eroded overnight... His tribulations did not end just there. He was ousted by his company's board and two of his female ex-colleagues slapped him with charges of sexual misconduct. His honour and reputation were shredded to bits in public, even before the courts could schedule the preliminary hearing for the case. And then this followed,' she said, pointing to the paper in Ronit's hand.

'Does the modus operandi sound familiar? A man at the helm of a successful business empire being pushed to the brink by a digital hack, losing his life in the end?'

'C K Ramanathan,' Ronit murmured. 'But this guy, Fei, didn't take his own life. It says he succumbed to a heart attack.'

'We don't believe he committed suicide either. When the rest of the world was busy looking for alternatives to aspirin, labs in Shandong and Wuhan were busy creating destructive viruses and untraceable poisons. Who knows…'

'And what does this have anything to do with this operative, Zhiming?'

'Zhiming is ruthless, guileful and potent. She is China's main weapon in their pursuit for global domination. She is the single most important factor behind the success that Operation Bamboo Garden has witnessed in recent years. She is prepared to scale any lengths of depravity to accomplish the tasks her masters entrust to her,' the viciousness of Noor's words revealed the spite and loathing she was nurturing for this agent, Zhiming.

'While she prefers to carry out the legwork of her operations on her own, she is backed by a team comprising the most proficient Chinese hackers. That explains why most of her operations are shaped in the digital as well as the real world. The death of Reng Fei was Zhiming's doing, as was Ramanathan's suicide. Before she arrived in India to target Ramanathan, another business empire in Hong Kong was reduced to rubble by her. If you study them closely, you will find several operational similarities in the manner that the three attacks were carried out in.'

Ronit's forehead was creased, and he was thinking

hard. 'But why Ramanathan? What could he have possibly done to become her target?' he almost murmured, as though his thoughts had somehow escaped from his lips.

'I told you earlier also, your country is under attack. You just don't know it yet. If Zhiming has been here for so long, she is no doubt orchestrating something big and momentous. Something that will compel your government into making unreasonable concessions for the Chinese. Ramanathan, for all you know, might have been a small cog in the wheel.'

Her words hit hard. There was a sincerity in her eyes that made Ronit want to believe her, but his vanity was standing in the way. India, his country, was the second most populous country in the world, and an emerging global superpower. It was no longer a cluster of fragmented kingdoms that the British had managed to rule for centuries. What could a lone Chinese agent do to bring such a powerful nation to its knees?

Ronit was himself a miniscule player in the security ranks of the country. He might have been hearing about Zhiming for the first time, but he was certain that there were others, more capable and powerful people who would be many steps ahead of him as well as his mysterious companion. If what Noor was saying were indeed true, these men and women of power would probably be observing Zhiming's actions on a big screen in a war room somewhere, laughing at her ignorance and naivete.

David taking on Goliath made for a fascinating story, but whoever had heard of David's puny toenail standing up to an entire mob of Goliaths? No, he, Ronit Biswas, was not meant to burden himself with matters of such gravity. These were things well beyond his paygrade. Afterall, he was nothing but a miniscule player.

'And just why do you need my help to track her? You seem pretty resourceful yourself, given the types of information you seem to have at your disposal each time we meet.'

'You are right. Apprehending Zhiming is the utmost priority for my government and me. My superiors have left no stone unturned to provide me with the resources I need to complete this job. However, there are limitations of access and speed while trying to track her from the outside. You, on the other hand, have the requisite clearances to access all networks, databases and systems of the country. You can run a query on the Customs and Immigrations databases to identify patterns, you can review their embassy personnel records for any anomalies and you can train your digital eyes to flag her off wherever she surfaces next. In short, if anyone can help us in catching Zhiming's scent, it is you.'

'Thank you! You make me sound more important than I am,' he returned awkwardly. 'But you said that you represent a friendly nation. So, why don't you approach our government through the standard channels? If you can substantiate all that you have told me, there is no reason why they will not be willing to cooperate with you. If the government decides to flex its muscles, Zhiming, no matter how slippery she is, will have nowhere to escape,' Ronit reasoned.

'Had that been a viable option, I wouldn't have been sitting here. Zhiming is in possession of something that is vital to my country's existence. Although this *thing* doesn't have anything to do with India, we can't let anyone, not even our allies, learn about it. We can still work with your authorities to apprehend her, but if she is captured on your soil, we will have no legitimate reason to seek an audience with her or to reclaim this thing from her. Even if your government wants it, international laws will prohibit them from granting us access to Zhiming while she remains in their custody.'

'But all this will be applicable even if I agree to help you and we end up apprehending her. Her detention will still be governed by international laws,' he interjected.

'That, Mr Biswas, is my only condition,' she said, a resolute glint twinkling in her eyes. 'Till such time that we are able to track Zhiming, you will involve no one in this project. Of course, you can assign specific tasks to members of your team, but you can't divulge anything beyond what they need to know and do. Involving any other security agency in her pursuit is out of the question. I will provide you with all the information you need, and you will use the digital firepower at your disposal to track her. And once you get wind of her, you will let me know.'

He let out a mocking laughter. 'That doesn't sound like two people pooling their resources to apprehend a common enemy. It is more like you attempting to use me and my department to get what you want. On your terms, of course.'

'It must sound like that, I am sure, but you need to see it for what it is. I need ten minutes of time alone with Zhiming before your people take her into custody. Ten minutes are all I need to get what I need from her—the thing that has remained my singular obsession for the past many months, the very reason why I am even here in your country right now. Beyond these ten minutes, I have no use of Zhiming. You can have her then. You can work on her to extract all the intelligence you need to protect your country against whatever her masters have tasked her to do. And you, Mr Biswas, will be the man to have unravelled the entire conspiracy. So, no, I am not using you for my ulterior motives, I am only presenting you with an opportunity to become a hero. For your country as well as mine.'

'Those are profound words, but why should I trust you. What if you intend to assassinate her and flee?'

'I would think I have given you enough reasons to trust me. At least forty-seven of them... But if you are still doubtful, once we apprehend her, lock the two of us someplace and call for backup in the meantime. Do all that you must to make sure that I have no way left to escape if I bring her any physical harm. What more can I say?' she replied, her words measured and purposeful.

'Okay, and what makes you think that you can trust me? I have all the information I need. I can simply refuse to help you, share everything with my own people and leave the task of tracking her to those who are trained to do it.'

It was Noor's turn to laugh now. 'Mr Biswas, this is Zhiming we are talking about. Your people aren't even aware of her presence in your country, let alone her identity. I am not questioning their competence, but we had an entire team of experts trying to trace her night and day. We knew what she looked like, and yet it took us nearly nine months to zero in on her location. I am not sure if you have the luxury of that kind of time… If you are to get to Zhiming before she causes any significant damage, I am your only hope.' Her lips curled into a smile as the words tailed.

'So you say, my dear, but wouldn't I be taking a considerable risk by joining hands with you? This whole thing could go anywhere. If Zhiming is as good as you say she is, there is a good chance that this whole thing might blow up on our faces. It will be safer for me to end this conversation right here and loop in my superiors. It will be up to the experts to prove their worth. At least I would have fulfilled my obligations and will be in the clear.'

Her smile widened ever so slightly. 'Mr Biswas, Zhiming might be a master of her trade, but I am no novice either. Give me some credit for having done my homework before I even approached you… I know how you think, how you work and what you stand for. In fact, it probably wouldn't be far from the truth if I said that I know you slightly better than you will ever know yourself… You will do no such thing, Mr Biswas, for if that is how you were programmed, you would have been sitting in a swanky office somewhere in Silicon Valley right now instead of trying to sip coffee from an empty cup…'

The coquetry was back in her voice now. Embarrassed, Ronit returned the cup to the table and reached out for the napkin. Noor burst out laughing once again.

'And let these not be mere words. Let me prove to you that I meant every word that I said,' she continued once the laughter had abated.

'You must believe, Mr Biswas, that the choice of this venue was your idea; that it was you who decided to get us here… You may even be right; you were driving the car after all, and you could have opted to take us anywhere. But why did we come exactly here? What if I told you that this wasn't entirely your doing, and that someone knew beforehand that we will be having this conversation right here, sipping coffee in this café on this very table?'

Ronit looked at her, puzzled. Her words had been making sense to him up until now, but then suddenly she had veered towards the ludicrous. He couldn't make head or tail of what she was suggesting now.

'Don't look so puzzled, Mr Biswas. All I am saying is that a thorough operative might have known precisely where we would be having this chat even before you decided to get us here. She would have gamed our conversation from the car and timed the point where we would agree to halt for coffee. She would know how much distance we would have covered by then, and accordingly, she would be able to identify the venue options you would need to choose from. If she has studied you well enough, she would put herself in your shoes, think like you would, and she would know that this is where you will eventually lead us.'

Noor's explanation did little to allay Ronit's confusion. He remained looking at her, his brows pulled up slightly to express his lack of comprehension.

'Okay, let it be… Let's call for the check. We should get going now… You can take your time to assimilate all you have heard, assess the situation, and message me once you've made up your mind. The encryption on my number is impenetrable, so you can message me anytime and anything that you feel like,' she said, punctuating the offer with a wink. Ronit felt something writhe in his gut. This is what made her irresistible, the ability to transform into an entirely different person within the space of a wink.

Containing a strong urge to make time pause, to keep listening to her tinkling laughter and words that effortlessly escaped her lips, Ronit raised his hand to catch the attention of the maître d'.

'Anything else, Sir?'

'No, please. Can you help us with the check instead?'

'Oh, but that has already been settled, Sir,' he said with a smile, his eyes glittering with the mischief of a co-conspirator.

'Madam had paid an advance to take care of the bill when she had come to reserve the table last evening.' With that, the man bowed and exited.

Noor had picked up her handbag and was ready to

leave too. However, Ronit was too stunned to even react. He remained occupying his seat, staring at the empty cup in disbelief.

'I have a car waiting for me,' Noor said, ruffling his hair with her hand, the smile still affixed on her face.

'We should do this more often, don't you think? I look forward to your message… till then, take care,' she said, before striding out of the coffee shop and through the hotel lobby.

Chapter 13

Roll Of The Dice

New Delhi, 6th January 2021

Ronit traversed the office floor and made for his cabin in a state of stupor. He missed acknowledging the random greetings that members of his team flung his way as he walked, leading to a few raised brows. Such was the impact of the last punch that Noor had delivered before staging a Houdini of sorts.

He had taken no more than a few seconds to gather his wits after she had left the coffee shop. As he emerged from his seat, he was certain that he had heard her distinct footsteps against the marble floor of the hotel lobby. He had walked briskly, taking rapid strides with the hope of catching up with her, but she was nowhere to be seen. Not in the hotel lobby and not in the portico. As he waited for the valet to fetch his car, his eyes remained darting hither-tither desirous of a single glimpse of the mystery that now had a name, but to no avail once again. Noor, it seemed, had walked straight into one of the hotel walls and had been swallowed by it in entirety.

As he surrendered himself to the chair in his cabin, a realisation dawned upon him: he had no option but to assist Noor in her pursuit. Her arguments, no doubt, were persuasive, but the clincher was the strong magnetism that was making it impossible for him to think of anything but her. She was a spy, a girl well trained in the art of deception, but there was something about her that made him want to believe her, to reveal his soul to her. This emotion had taken siege of Ronit's being and it was starting to shadow his thoughts. He knew that he had to meet her again, and the only way he could make this happen was by agreeing to work with her.

The only thing left for Ronit to do was to convey his decision to her. Which anyway seemed like a formality, given the certainty with which she was able to predict his actions.

Ronit chose to wait. He was like a pugilist who continues to fight despite the scoreboard leaving no opening for him to steal a victory. It was a battle of honour, and he was not going to lose by knockout. He could reveal his soul to her, but not his desperation. Like the pugilist, he would bide time, he would make her wait in anticipation, he would go down, but on his feet and not on his knees. The conclusion was foregone, but he would put off her victory lap for as long as he could. Whenever he met her, he would meet her as an equal, a partner and not someone who had been coerced into submission.

His resolve powered him to navigate more than half the day, albeit without getting much work done. Ronit had found it impossible to focus on work while dealing with the tug of war that was waging within him. The only thing he managed to accomplish was a supposedly objective evaluation of Noor's proposal to back the decision that he had already arrived at.

Even if what Noor had told him was half true, getting to Zhiming had to be the first step towards unravelling her larger plan. She might or might not be embroiled in a plot as damning as Noor had made it sound, but Zhiming was a Chinese spy operational on Indian soil, nonetheless. If nothing, her detention was bound to ring in laurels and accolades for Ronit.

On the other hand, if they didn't succeed—well, if they were unable to track her, why did anybody have to know that they were even trying to do so? There was nothing he stood to lose even if things were to go southwards.

It was sometime in the late afternoon when Ronit, having legitimised the decision in his own eyes, reached out for his phone.

'I will help you, but I will need more details to start work. Can we meet?' he typed. After reading the message twice over, he deleted it. It was too blatant, too forthright, too revealing.

It was in the fourth attempt that he was able to string together words that finally read right. He wrote, 'We can work together, but only if you tell me the details of what you need from her. Trust works both ways, right?'

'That's a fair ask... I will... At the right time,' the reply came instantly.

'Can you share the picture? I can initiate the groundwork before you provide me more specifics to plan the pursuit,' he wrote.

This time it took him only two attempts to get the message right. He was getting good at it. This was his well-concealed hook to draw her into meeting him again.

This time Ronit's phone did not chime as swiftly as it had done previously. He remained staring at the screen, his heart scuffling to make an escape via his oral tract. It finally settled in its ordained place when the phone announced the arrival of two back-to-back messages.

She had sent him two pictures, ostensibly of the same woman, clicked at different points in time. One was a grainy photograph, quite like a screengrab from a low-resolution CCTV camera, with the backdrop so out of focus that it was impossible to tell where it had been captured. The other one was a much better capture, clicked inside an airport in India. Which one, he couldn't tell.

Ronit was still studying the photographs when another message arrived. 'I will reach out soon,' it said. Ronit had started to type a reply, but he stopped himself midsentence and deleted what he had written. With considerable effort, he had succeeded in turning the tide. He was engaging with Noor on his terms now, his faults and vulnerabilities concealed well from her, and he had no intentions of letting the situation slip out of hand once again.

He did consider that he might be overcompensating, at least in this one instance, but Ronit was quick to shrug the thought off. Instead, he got busy decrypting the picture files and transferring them to his laptop.

He was going to meet Noor soon. He wasn't sure when, but he knew that she could turn up anywhere and anytime. Only, this time he was going to be better prepared for the meeting.

With Zhiming's pictures, he could create match alerts in all sorts of security feeds and databases, especially the CCTV captures at obvious places such as airports and toll plazas. He could even scan the stored feeds from the past few days with the hope of finding a match. However, that would draw out most of the server bandwidth at his disposal, something he was authorised to do, but couldn't achieve without raising several eyebrows. Moreover, finding a match could take any amount of time. There was no way for him to control that.

Ronit needed something, anything, on Zhiming, before he faced Noor again. And to enable this, an efficacious route was to search databases that were meant to capture particulars of foreign nationals visiting the country—immigration logs and visa issuance records. Zhiming, Noor had mentioned, wasn't the Chinese operative's real name, but that didn't matter. The records in these databases would be finite and a simple facial recognition query could throw up results within a matter of days, hours if he was lucky.

The access for these records was restricted, but Ronit,

in his official capacity, had been accorded the requisite clearances needed to scan them. In fact, every now and then his department had to run such queries as part of their ongoing investigations. Hence, his action wasn't likely to draw any unwarranted attention.

It took him all of twenty minutes to run a query for matching the pictures he had received against those on the files of all approved visa applications and arrivals from China in the past two months. A smaller timeframe would yield the results faster, and if he didn't find a match, he could always extend the time horizon. He was hoping that the search would have yielded some results by the time he returned to office the next morning.

Unable to concentrate on much else, Ronit returned home early. Ritualistically, Barkha brought him his tea, which he sipped in relative silence.

He was close to emptying his cup when Barkha's phone rang. She excused herself to the bedroom and remained chatting with the caller for the next 40 minutes. Her intermittent laughter continued to reach his ears despite the half-shut door. Ronit had an inkling as to who the caller might be, but somehow, he didn't find this knowledge to be as disturbing as it should have been. He went about the rest of the evening, aloof, nearly indifferent to the surroundings, lost in a maze of his own thoughts.

It was shortly after dinner, when he was flipping through news channels, that his phone rang. Instead of the caller's name or phone number, his screen displayed 'Undisclosed Number'. Ronit looked at the screen for a moment before receiving the call.

'Hello, are you at home right now?' he heard Noor's unmistakable voice on the line. She sounded rushed and perturbed.

'Yes, what happened?'

'Listen carefully. You need to get out of there right away… I will explain later. Just get out of the house, walk past where you had parked your car yesterday, and turn left once you cross the small playground. A little ahead there is a big tree on the roadside. Wait for me there. I should be reaching in ten to fifteen minutes. And remember, stand close to the tree. Don't step beyond three or four metres from the trunk while you are waiting there,' she sputtered in a single breath.

'I don't get this…,' Ronit started to speak, but was mercilessly interrupted mid-sentence.

'I will explain later. Now, hurry… there's no time to waste,' she said, before the beep of a disconnected call rang in his ears.

Noor's tone did not leave much scope for Ronit to procrastinate. It took him about five minutes to reach the suggested vantage point. Once there, the stupidity of his situation dawned upon him. Following the instructions of a girl he had met just twice, and who he knew was a foreign spy, he had stepped out of his house at night without even bothering to inform his wife.

He had no idea where he was headed and why. For now, he was standing outside a now empty playground, under an overgrown tree, waiting to discover the reasons that would justify his actions to his own self.

If any resident of the nearby flats happened to peep out, all they would see was the silhouette of a suspicious character lurking in the neighborhood. Realising that this could lead to an alarm being raised, he pulled out his phone and started scanning his social media feeds. Though his eyes kept darting back to the road, this was the best he could do to look purposeful and occupied.

Ronit's wait proved shorter than what he had been told, by his own estimation at least, for soon a black Hyundai Verna appeared at the turn. It came straight at him and halted with a screech barely a few steps away. He bent down and peered inside to get a look at the driver, but the angle of the streetlights made it difficult.

'Hurry, get in,' he heard Noor shout out. On cue, he opened the passenger side door and got inside.

'Here, put these on,' she said, handing him a cap and a windcheater. 'Try not to look up while we are on the road. And switch off your phone too.'

Ronit was in the intelligence business alright, but this whole cloak and dagger affair was altogether new to him. Somewhat frightening too. He followed Noor's instructions without voicing a protest. Noor glanced at his modified look and satisfied, she set the car into motion.

For the next several minutes they remained racing on the streets of Delhi with the steady drone of the running engine and sporadic honks from other irate drivers being the only sounds to reach their ears.

'Can we talk now? What is this all about?' unable to

contain his anxiety, Ronit eventually broke the silence.

'What did you do with the pictures I sent you? Did you run a search query on any public database to find a match for them?' she returned with a set of questions of her own.

'I did run a query, but not on public databases. I was looking for a match on the immigration and visa records. Why? What happened?'

'Well, for starters you can blame me for acting on impulse and not having gamed this scenario… I really needed your support on this case, and when you agreed to work with me, I didn't suppose it was wise to deny you the one thing you had asked for—Zhiming's pictures. Of course, I intended to connect with you tomorrow morning to chart out our next steps. I wasn't expecting you to get into action so soon, but I doubt if things would have been any different if we had started our search a day later. I mean, how could either of us have known the extent to which they have already penetrated your systems?' her eyes were affixed on the road, and she seemed to be thinking out aloud, the worry in her words clearly discernible.

'Will you tell me what happened?' Ronit shot out, nervousness beginning to weigh in on him. 'This gibberish is not making much sense to me.'

'What has happened, Mr Biswas, is that Zhiming is on to you. She knows that you are in possession of her pictures and are trying to dig more information about her.'

'How is that even possible? I ran the query on highly

secure databases...,' Ronit began to respond, but was interrupted mid-sentence by Noor.

'Mr Biswas, Zhiming is not any ordinary operative. She has an entire team of accomplished hackers, some of the best in the business, supporting every one of her operations. They would have set up alerts on most digital networks to warn them of unexpected activities concerning areas that they are interested in... I must admit, though, that I hadn't expected them to have infiltrated the security of servers that store the records that you are mentioning. And that should tell you something not only of their reach and abilities, but also of the magnitude of the threat that your country is facing.'

Ronit took his time to assimilate what he had just heard. 'How do you know all this?' he eventually asked, lowering his voice considerably.

'We have our own eyes and ears plugged into cyberspace too. Just like the Chinese, we monitor the keywords that we are interested in, and you, Mr Biswas, certainly qualify for someone we, or at least I am keenly interested in,' she began. If she were insinuating something, Ronit allowed it to pass.

'About an hour back we got an unusually high number of pings against your name. On probing further, we found that a concerted cyberattack had been mounted against you by a group of China affiliated hackers. We will know in some time as to what specific areas they intend to hit or the extent of damage they plan to cause, but it is certain that they are coming for you... Of what I know about

Zhiming's ways, they will look to discredit you—perhaps turn your own government against you—so that anything you might have gathered against her loses all credibility. This will only be an immediate damage control tactic though. In the long run, they will seek to eliminate you. The Chinese, and especially Zhiming, doesn't believe in leaving loose ends…'

Noor had spoken matter-of-factly. She could very well have been reading out a bedtime story to a toddler. Ronit, on the other hand, had his heart in his mouth. He couldn't think of anything to say. He was like a man who had just been informed that one of the most powerful nations in the world had just trained an entire team of covert operatives upon him. Not only were they out to eliminate him, but his own country wasn't going to protect him either.

'You got me into this,' he nearly screamed, letting his frustrations get the better of him. 'Now you need to get me out too… Tell me, what will we do? Should we reach out to someone in the Chinese embassy and tell them that the search query was run by mistake… a technical glitch or something?'

'Ronit, you are not thinking clearly… Let us get to our destination and figure out what the Chinese are up to. We will find a way out of this. The very reason I am here with you right now is that you are in this mess because of me. And trust me, I will get you out of it too…,' as her words tailed, she shot him another glance. This time he saw compassion, concern and a steely resolve in her eyes.

It was awkwardly comforting. Or perhaps he was just a drowning man clutching at the straws he could see.

Ronit continued soaking in the precariousness of his situation for some time before he spoke meekly. 'Where are we going? And how is all this going to help us?' he said, tugging at the lapel of the windcheater.

'We are going someplace secure, a safehouse in standard trade parlance, and this is to make sure that no one identifies you, now or even later. If Zhiming has her way, your official agencies will soon be mounting a manhunt for you. Her people will be looking for you too, if they aren't already on the way to your home… For whatever it is worth, it is the latter that we should be more concerned about. Anyways, what do you think they will do once they find you missing from home?'

'Try to trace my phone?'

'Precisely,' she said, giving him the glance that a proud teacher would reserve for her star student.

'And they would scan the cameras, public and private, that might have captured your escape. They will know exactly what to look for and around what time, so without the right precautions it will be a matter of time before they spot you sitting in this car. I don't need to tell you how long it will take for them to chart out the entire travel map for the car, including its destination… And the one thing I can surely do without is somebody turning up at the safehouse in the middle of the night to disturb my sleep.'

Sleep was the farthest thing on Ronit's mind right

now. His thoughts were darting across a million things and none of them remotely resembled a comfortable bed.

He refrained from voicing his opinion though, preferring instead to slip back into the comforting embrace of silence. With all the turmoil brewing within him, speaking was anyway becoming an increasingly arduous task. He would take another shot at it once they had safely made it to their destination.

Chapter 14

The Exploration

New Delhi, 6th January 2021

The city of Delhi was changing, and it was changing at a rapid pace. The past ten months had not only tested the city's resilience, but it had led to marked shifts in the way of life of its residents. With human beings holed up within their homes for the most part, some gripped by fear and others driven by compulsion, nature had found the time it needed to heal itself. The air had lost its pungency, and the streets looked agreeable and almost inviting.

To Ronit, though, the roads were nothing more than concrete arteries serving the very specific task of ferrying essentials to keep the rest of the body alive. He remained looking at them, devoid of any romanticism they might have evoked another time, trying to make sense of his situation. The course of his life had suddenly taken a macabre turn, resembling grim poetry from the Victorian era.

Noor was commandeering the vehicle with the audacity and brazenness of a seasoned Delhi driver. Perhaps an attempt to prevent the car from standing out among other vehicles on the road.

'Anonymity is not about doing the customary or the expected. It is all about aping what those around you are doing, no matter how absurd their actions might seem to you. A sane man surrounded by members of a doomsday cult intent on ending their lives will but stick out like a sore thumb,' he recalled having heard somewhere.

They had travelled along the Outer Ring Road, past IIT Delhi—his alma mater—before turning towards Gurugram. Around Chhatarpur, they had taken a sharp left on a road barely wide enough to accommodate two crossing cars. Within minutes the smooth metaled road had metamorphosed into a broken, potholed one, and the density of houses on both sides had been rapidly reduced.

The headlights of the vehicle were now their only source of illumination, making Ronit realise that the civic authorities had not bothered to erect light poles on the road. The tawny light emanating from the buildings around them had given them a feeling of driving through habitation, but all that had changed with the sudden turn.

With no other vehicles in sight, surrounded mostly by intermittent boundary walls and dense foliage, and habited structures few and far between, they could have been driving anywhere in the rural heartland of the country. This hardly seemed like the Delhi that Ronit had known. And yet, Noor was racing down the winding, bumpy road with the familiarity of someone who had been living in these parts forever. Ronit noticed that she hadn't needed any assistance with the navigation thus far. He wondered where they were, perhaps some isolated section of Chhatarpur Farms, and he wondered whether a GPS enabled navigation app would even work in these remote environs.

'We are almost there,' she said, taking a sudden turn onto a dirt track that Ronit had failed to notice earlier. The jerk did well to jolt him back to reality. After a few yards, they were greeted by a large metal gate, which stood in their path.

Noor stopped the car, and with the engine still running, stepped down to open the gate. Once inside what appeared to be a large, gated compound, she repeated her actions to shut the gate behind them. They drove for another couple of minutes to arrive at a small single-floor structure concealed between a clump of large trees. She stopped the car and killed the engine, signalling Ronit to disembark. He abided, stepping out in the dark, able to see little and comprehend even lesser.

Noor opened the trunk and pulled out a car cover. Ronit remained frozen, too befuddled to extend a helping hand as she wrapped the plastic around the vehicle.

'Come,' she said, leading him to the wooden door. By the time Ronit stepped inside, she had switched on a low wattage bulb. It was a small but adequately furnished living room with a flatscreen TV surrounded by comfortable settees, a bookshelf and framed paintings adorning the walls. The adornments were expensive, but not necessarily meant to complement each other. They were possibly picked up one item at a time, with utility and not aesthetics being the driver of choice.

Noor stepped forward to draw the curtains on the large glass door to the far side. To Ronit's left was a small passage leading to an open kitchen, and to his right were two half-open wooden doors.

'This is the bedroom,' Noor said, pushing one of the doors open. Ronit stepped forward to catch a glimpse. It was a small room with a double bed, side tables and a wall mounted wardrobe. While the hall had exhibited some traces of habitation—a faint cocktail of human aromas and the random article out of its designated place—the bedroom was quite a different sight. With garments flung carelessly, Noor's size and type mostly, crumpled bedlinen, and a floor littered with discarded footwear, it appeared to have been ravaged by a storm of considerable magnitude.

'And that, there, is the washroom,' Noor continued unfazed, pointing to the door that opened into the attached bathroom.

'And this,' she said, shifting her attention to the second door, 'is the study cum spare room.' Ronit stepped behind her to find a largely unadorned space, but for the wooded table on which two laptops lay, surrounded by four office chairs. The room resembled a makeshift conference facility, which by the random positioning of the chairs seemed to have been vacated in a hurry.

'It might not be the Ritz Carlton, but this place has almost everything that one might need for a few days of relatively austere living. Moreover, it is away from prying eyes and as safe a place as any you might find in Delhi. What do you think of it?'

Her words could have been a subtle attempt to sell the safehouse and the idea that Ronit was going to have to call it home for the time being, but her guest's mind was meandering elsewhere. 'How long will I have to stay here? I didn't even inform Barkha while leaving the house, and now my phone is switched off too… She would be worried.'

Noor looked back at him, with a smile that seemed to appreciate his naivete, like a kindergarten teacher would respond to an innocent question by one of her students. 'Mr Biswas, if I were you, my wife's anxiety would be the least of my concerns,' she said, extending her hand to ruffle the hair on his head.

'Let us first try and get our minds around what they are up to,' she said, reaching out for one of the laptops, plugging it out of the charging port and stepping out into the living room. She parked herself on the settee, busying herself with the laptop keys. Hesitantly, Ronit sat down beside her and affixed his gaze on the tabs appearing on the screen.

'Look at this,' pointing to a news article that had just popped up.

Ronit was already reading the headline. It said, 'India's Vaccine Programme in Jeopardy: Details of the Covid-19 vaccine storage facilities and distribution plan leaked.' The article had been published by a digital news portal which was a known baiter of the current dispensation. As Ronit read the detailed report, his eyes widened with a mix of disbelief, anger and a chilling gush of fear.

The article outlined how the Prime Minister had announced that one of the world's largest vaccination drive would kickstart in the country in another five days. The government, it explained, had prepared a detailed blueprint on how the vaccines would move from the six central godowns to state warehouses first, and then to the thousands of vaccination centres, while strictly maintaining the prescribed storage temperatures. There were intelligence reports in the public domain to suggest that certain unscrupulous elements might attempt to rob the vaccines during transit, so their storage and transportation plan had been kept under wraps.

'We have learnt through credible sources that the details of facilities where the vaccines are stored as well as the schedule of their transportation has been leaked. Pakistani and Chinese secret services are said to have acquired this information through a mole in the Indian Intelligence Wing (RAD). The mole is a senior official of RAD who enjoys the highest levels of security clearance. We are in possession of a copy of the email sent from this official's personal email id with the detailed vaccination programme blueprint to his foreign handlers.'

The story, without naming Ronit, had gone on to provide details that left little doubt in the minds of an informed reader about the identity of the mole. It was he, Ronit, who was being blamed for having compromised a programme on which possibly millions of lives depended. They claimed to be in possession of the email that was responsible for the leak. An email that he had purportedly sent from his personal id.

The news article went on to question the government's management of this crucial initiative and their approach to national security in general, but Ronit's vision had started blurring already. He finished reading the article, not registering much of the later sections, before looking at Noor. 'What is all this?'

'This is the way they work; you shouldn't be surprised… The silver lining is that we now know what they are trying to pin on you, and we can figure out what needs to be done to prevent it,' she said without looking back at him. Her eyes were still glued to the laptop screen.

'I am not surprised!' Ronit burst out, tears trickling down his eyes, 'I am… I am… I don't even know what I am feeling right now. Till this evening I was a respected man with some social standing, with a career dedicated to serving my country. And here I am, barely a few hours later, being branded a traitor… A despicable man who has sold his country to its enemies… What have I done to deserve this?'

Ronit had covered his face with his palms and was convulsing audibly. Noor eyed him for a few moments, able to understand his agony but unsure of how to react. For someone who felt more comfortable in a boxing ring than a family dinner table, the setting was anything but agreeable for her. Placing the laptop on the centre table, she cautiously extended her arms and wrapped them around Ronit. Ronit didn't object, instead he tilted his head to let it rest on Noor's shoulder and she let her fingers slip into his hair, tenderly massaging his scalp. They held their positions for a long time, trying to make sense of the multitude of emotions that each one was experiencing, until Ronit was able to gather himself and pull his head back up.

The strongest of human bonds are formed not when we are able to impress someone through the projection of a commanding and authoritative persona, but when we expose our vulnerabilities and weaknesses in their presence. The sight of a real, blemished person sometimes does what the glitter of a shiny armour is not able to.

In their time on the settee, sitting side by side, both Noor and Ronit experienced an intimacy, a kinship that otherwise would have been impossible to find in the little time that they had known each other.

'My mentor used to say that how we emerge from a situation is ten percent about the gravity of the situation itself and ninety percent about how we respond to it. We are going to come out of this, trust me!'

'I know you mean well but forgive me if I find myself unable to share your optimism,' Ronit returned, putting on a smile that failed to reach his eyes.

'You know, when I was a child my grandfather would tell me stories of our brave freedom fighters—Bhagat

Singh, Khudiram Bose, Surya Sen, Chandrasekhar Azad… Later I would play out these stories in my head, replacing the principal characters with my own self. I would imagine myself hurling bombs on the parliament floor, I would see myself in the Azad Park exchanging fire with the constabulary, and I would even visualise the hangman covering my head and securing the noose around my neck. Eventually I realised that I was probably inspired by the pride and passion with which my grandfather narrated these tales, and privately I would fantasise about becoming the source of similar pride for him and my family. I was just an impressionable child, you know…'

Noor listened intently, not following the references to the Indian freedom struggle but opting not to interject.

'This emotion turned out to be far more deep-rooted than I had imagined. When the option of joining RAD came my way, it was this urge to serve my country, to bring pride to my family that shaped my decision. The job was very different from what I had been preparing for, but I enjoyed it, all the same. It seemed to serve some higher objective for me… And now, all that is gone in a single flash. I am being called a traitor, a mole… Today it is one publication, tomorrow it will be the 24-hour news channels and then the social media. My reputation and my character will be slain over and over again…,' he said, pausing abruptly when he felt moisture building up in his eyes again.

Noor reached out and held his hand. 'I can't pretend

to understand all that you are feeling, but believe me when I say that we will emerge from this unscathed. All we need to do is figure out a way to get to Zhiming before she gets to you. We will prevent her from achieving her nefarious objectives, and once you bring her in, you will become a hero. The same news channels that you are worrying about today will be clamouring to interview you then.'

'And how exactly are we going to do that? You yourself said that your agency had been tracking her for several months and all you have to show for it is a couple of pictures. How do you suppose the two of us are going to get to her before she strikes?'

'You know, this game is quite like a game of soccer,' she said after a thoughtful pause. 'When a team gets on the offensive, the cracks in its defence also begin to show. This is when their opponents have the best chance of scoring. Zhiming is on the offensive now. The opening will present itself soon. We need to be prepared to shoot when it does.'

'And till then we keep hiding here like fugitives, letting her wreak havoc in my life?' he argued.

'No, we don't,' she returned calmly. 'We need to be proactive, we need to act, but our actions need to be meticulously planned. The margin for error is going to be wafer thin. We can't afford even a single wrong move at this stage. It could cost us dearly.'

'The motivational spiel is all fine, but what exactly are you proposing we do? I made a straightforward attempt to track her and see where it has landed us. And that was when I had legitimate access to all of RAD's resources. How do you think we are going to better that while being on the run?' he countered.

'I don't have an answer to that. At this point I don't even know what we should do, but I am sure that if we put our heads together, we will come up with a solution. Only, I don't think either of us are in a state to do so now.'

Noor waited for Ronit to respond, but he didn't. Instead, he continued to look at her, leaving her with no option but to elaborate her point.

'My mentor had this technique—the Zen approach, he called it—which is by far the most effective thing that I have picked up from him. He said that when you are faced with an overwhelming situation, your faculties get preoccupied in managing the emotional reactions it elicits. If you push yourself for answers just then, the direction your thoughts take will be dictated not by objectivity and prudence, but by your dominant emotions. This is a trap, like a quicksand. The harder you push, the deeper you will sink, and the solution that will emerge will be suboptimal at best.'

She paused to assess if Ronit was being able make sense of her reasoning. He appeared to be listening attentively. Satisfied, she continued, 'The right thing to do in such situations is to mentally detach yourself from them for a little while. This is not simple, sometimes it might even take a strong distraction to be able to do so, but it clears your mind and allows you to approach the issue afresh later. You find yourself better able to think of possibilities and eventualities that might not even have occurred to you earlier. And that is when you truly seize control of the situation instead of allowing the situation to control your actions.'

'So, are you suggesting that we go to sleep now and approach it with a fresh mind in the morning? Like it is a mathematics assignment that we are trying to solve... Do you really think that I will be able to put all this aside and get myself a good night's sleep?' he said, his words dripping with unintended sarcasm.

'Yes, I do think that we should get back to this in the morning. This might not be a math assignment, but you will still do well to tackle it when you are at your sharpest... As I said, it is not going to be easy, but you will need to find a way to distract yourself for now,' she said. 'How about dinner? Should I get you something to eat? I am sure you must be starving,' she added, glancing at her wristwatch.

He couldn't help but smile at her earnest but amateurish attempt to divert his thoughts. 'I was done with my dinner long before an unexpected phone call brought the ceiling crashing down on my head... but thank you!'

'Shouldn't you be thanking the caller for warning you of the impending disaster just in time?' she replied, shrinking her eyes to feign an indignant look. 'Let's do whiskey then! It might also help you catch a shut-eye later.'

Following Ronit's consenting nod, she made for the kitchen and resurfaced with two glasses and a half-filled bottle of Glenfiddich 12 Year Old. She disappeared for a second time, for a slightly longer duration, and returned with an ice bucket and a bowl of roasted peanuts.

'To the unexpected caller,' she said, unable to come up with anything more appropriate to raise a toast for. Ronit picked up his own drink, and touching the tip of the glass with hers, he returned, 'to the caller.'

Noor was determined not to let his internal gloom consume Ronit. She went about sharing stories of the strange people and circumstances she had encountered in her line of work, without getting into operational specifics of course. To engage Ronit, she even peppered her narration with cues and questions for him to respond. Ronit was participative, but only to the extent that civility demanded. He was clearly unable to let go of the burden that was weighing him down. Instead, his focus remained on liberally ingesting alcohol into his system.

He had emptied the last drops from the bottle into his glass, his fourth large drink while Noor was still finishing her second. 'Don't worry, there is more where that came from,' Noor said, noticing his gaze alternating between the empty bottle in his hand and her. She took one last swig to empty her own glass and returned to the kitchen to usher in additional supplies.

By the time she came back, Ronit had claimed the remote and put on a news channel on the TV, the volume muted of course. The ticker at the bottom of the screen was flashing nuggets about the ongoing farmers' protest and the political posturing around the upcoming vaccination drive. There was no mention of any information leak or RAD. Not yet at least!

'No!' Noor very nearly screamed upon noticing what he was up to. 'The TV is not going to help… You need to switch it off.'

Ronit, instead of acting on her directive, extended the hand holding the remote towards her. She claimed it wordlessly and turned off the TV. She poured herself another drink, and after depositing herself beside him, said, 'It is not working, is it? What can I do to keep you from thinking about it? Wait, I have an idea!'

She returned the glass to the table, and nearly jumped up from the settee. 'How about a lap dance?' she said, wiggling her hips suggestively. 'Now if this won't get you interested, I am not sure if anything will,' she added, winking wickedly.

Her act and her persistent attempt to cheer him up brought a smile to Ronit's face. 'Don't underestimate yourself. A lap dance by you should be enough to rouse the dead, and I am still breathing,' he found himself saying.

'Is that so?' she asked suggestively, putting a foot on the settee, and bending forward to bring her face close to his. With narrow eyes, she ran the back of her index finger across his cheek.

As she withdrew, her fingers brushed against Ronit's lips, and he felt a spark ignite somewhere deep inside his body. He knew that Noor was only playing the part of a seductress, but he couldn't stop his eyelids from closing and his lips from parting ever so slightly. It was an irrepressible reflex that didn't go unnoticed by his host.

Noor, perhaps driven by an impulse of her own, leaned towards him once again and planted her own lips on his. The entire sequence played out within a matter of seconds, not giving them time to ruminate or check their actions. The alcohol in their bloodstreams might have played the role of a catalyst too, but it was difficult to tell.

The union of their lips released an imperceptible tension that had been lingering in the air all evening. The kiss was like the spark that had unwittingly started a wildfire.

Noor sitting on his lap, holding his face in her hands as if it were a delicious fruit that she couldn't get enough of, and Ronit propped on the couch, his arms hungrily wrapped around her, was soon the scene in the living room of the safe house. For the next several minutes they remained on the sofa, their bodies entangled, hands exploring and lips locked.

Ronit hadn't experienced in a long time what he was experiencing now. Zhiming, the news article and even Barkha were but a distant blur in his memory for the time being. All that mattered in the moment was Noor. He wanted to feel and etch each crevice, every contour of her body on the canvas of his mind. Her smell, the feel of her hair brushing against him—he wanted to bottle up each sensation for posterity, and he went about collecting them meticulously.

Their garments, one after the other, began to form a

heap on the floor until their torsos were covered only by each other's skin.

'It's cold here... You want to head inside?' she whispered softly into his ears, nibbling on the lobe as she did so. It took Ronit's brain a few seconds to emerge from its engrossment and process the request.

He pulled himself to his feet without separating her body from his. What was transpiring between them was magnificent and precious. He couldn't risk an interruption, for who knew if the moment would ever return in its full glory once it had passed. So, with her legs wrapped around his waist, their bodies rubbing against each other, Ronit carried Noor inside the bedroom.

The wrinkled sheet and scattered clothing no longer held any meaning. The moment was all about two thirsty souls seeking bliss and contentment in each other's arms.

Chapter 15

The Wheels Are Turning

New Delhi, 7th January 2021

Ronit woke up feeling disoriented and muddled. The surroundings were unfamiliar, and he had to pause and think about the sequence of events that had led him here.

Then, in a sudden flash, everything started coming back to him. His already throbbing head turned into a vortex of random thoughts and recollections, which came rushing in from all directions: The unexpected phone call, the drive to the safehouse and the news article. He was gripped by an intense feeling of fear, and he felt his heart thudding against his chest.

He shut his eyes again and held his head tightly between his palms. The sharp tearing pain made him feel like his skull was about to explode.

He remained still for a while before suddenly realising that Noor was not on the bed beside him. Upon training his ears, he thought he could hear some activity in the living area. She had probably woken up before him and decided to get on with her day.

As he thought about her, a fresh set of memories from the preceding night returned. Their conversation, her offer of a lap dance and all that followed thereafter. It had been a surreal experience for Ronit. The love making had been passionate and tiring, and yet it had been fulfilling in some strange way. The recollections came with flashing images and Ronit felt the blood supply in his body rush to a totally different focal point. He had to manipulate his thoughts to control his bodily reactions.

Was it even for real? The sweet nothings she whispered in his ears, did she actually mean them, or were they a part of her ploy to distract him from the situation he faced?

Instantly, he hated himself for allowing the appalling thought to even surface. 'She is a spy alright, but that doesn't make her devoid of human emotions. She is helping you enough already, there was no need for her to go to such lengths just to make you feel better. If she didn't really care for you, she could have left you to your own desolate designs,' a voice inside his head argued, chiding him for his cynicism and suspicion.

He tried thinking about Noor in a different light, and surprisingly he felt embarrassed. It was the morning-after awkwardness of someone who had remained a one-woman-man for a better part of his life. Now that he had stepped beyond the boundaries of familiarity, he was hesitant and indecisive. He wasn't sure what he would say to Noor when he saw her, or how he would bring himself to face her.

Ronit hadn't even overcome the fear of facing Noor when his thoughts steered themselves in an entirely different direction, as though they had acquired a mind of their own. The face of Barkha, his wife, flashed before his eyes and he felt a sharp stab of guilt pierce through his innards. Of course, he was guilty of having been with another woman, but the fact that he had failed to inform her of his whereabouts was way more damning. He had not only been adulterous, but also irresponsible and inconsiderate.

The prevailing tensions in their marital life had made their incorporeal commitments take a backseat, but she was still his companion and thus had every right to be kept in the know of his whereabouts. He had simply left the house and not returned all night. She might have tried to reach him, but his phone had been switched off too. If he were in her place, he would have been frantically calling all her friends and acquaintances by now. Barkha would be worried and anxious, and her condition was only going to worsen once she learnt about the allegations being levelled against him.

No matter how hard he tried, Ronit was unable to justify his doings even to himself. The nagging voice in his head was already screaming its lungs out in protest. 'You had no business subjecting her to the agony of uncertainty and ignorance. Ask yourself, did you even make a sincere effort to reach out to her? The phone being switched off is a feeble excuse, and you know that perfectly well. If you were sincere, you could have thought of a hundred different ways to contact Barkha.'

Ronit tried to reason with the voice, but gave up soon. It was way too logical and persistent for his liking. Instead, he turned on his side and got out of the bed in measured movements. There was a lot happening in his life, and the luxury of staying put in bed to nurse a hangover or to argue with a voice that no one else could hear was not something he could afford.

Dragging himself to the washroom, he bolted the door behind him. Later, when he emerged, he looked in much better shape than before. The headache still lingered, but he was walking normally now and the creases on his forehead had reduced drastically.

'Good morning,' Noor greeted him as he stepped out of the bedroom. She was perched on the sofa, her laptop lying precariously on the armrest, supported only by a touch of her left hand.

'Good morning,' he returned, trying to match her beaming smile. And just like that, within a matter of seconds, the wall of hesitations he had erected around him stood demolished. His apprehensions about how he would face Noor turned out to be baseless, and he was relieved.

'There's some black coffee in the kettle,' she said, pointing towards the kitchen. 'I think it will do you good! Also, there are eggs and toast in case you are hungry… I am sorry, I didn't know by what time you will get up, so I went ahead with my breakfast.'

Ronit was in no mood to eat, but the coffee he couldn't

refuse. He poured himself a cup before joining her.

'She's not targeting the vaccination programme,' Noor looked up from the screen and said to him with a sense of definiteness. Ronit had a few things simmering in his own head that he wanted to bring up, so he didn't latch on to the context immediately.

'Zhiming,' she added in response to his puzzled look. 'She's not looking to disrupt India's vaccination drive. It is just a smokescreen meant to divert our attention. She is targeting something else.'

'Could be, but how does that even matter? The fact that the vaccination programme might be a target is probably known to half the world by now. If they haven't changed the entire storage and transportation plan already, they will probably do so anytime. The security would be beefed up to unimaginable levels, making it impossible for Zhiming or any other miscreant to set foot within miles of the vaccines,' he replied almost nonchalantly.

'Precisely! If the Chinese were planning to disrupt the programme, the last thing they would do is to put it under the spotlight themselves and make their own job more difficult,' she returned.

'I have been analysing the situation and there are several indicators that suggest that they might be aiming for an entirely different target. For instance, the world is still debating whether China is to blame for the Covid-19 outbreak. Imagine how it would impact their global image if they were found guilty of interfering with India's efforts to vaccinate its citizens against the very same virus. No, this is not a chance that Beijing will be willing to take.'

'I wouldn't bet on the Chinese losing sleep over what the rest of the world thinks of them, but you have a point. I don't think that the vaccine programme is at risk either,' Ronit conceded, before shifting tracks to his own agenda. 'Hey, since my phone can't be switched on, is there a phone here that I could use?'

'Oh yes,' she said, setting her laptop aside and getting up from the couch. 'I will get you a burner phone. The handset does not have a registered IMEI number, so you can make calls without the risk of getting tracked. I don't think I need to tell you, but you shouldn't call any of your family members or close colleagues. All their numbers will be under surveillance, and if they intercept you on a live call, it will be a piece of cake for them to zero in on our location.'

Ronit nodded, without letting his disappointment show. He was hoping to call Barkha to let her know that he was fine and that the accusations against him were all baseless. In his enthusiasm he had forgotten that unlike the movies where a conversation had to persist for a few minutes for the location of the caller to be traced, there were technologies available that could track the call to its tower of origin within a matter of seconds. Even burner phones that called or received calls from numbers under surveillance were at equal risk of discovery.

He was aware that in metro cities such as Delhi, mobile towers were usually placed at a gap of one to two kilometres. This meant that a tower responds to signals from mobile phones within a radius of half kilometre or slightly more, beyond which the phone would get connected to the next tower. The difficulty in locating an individual in a half kilometre radius was directly proportional to the density of population in the area. In most parts of the city this would imply combing through at least a few thousand dwellings and investigating an even larger number of people. But the story of their present location was different. The seclusion, which augured well for the safehouse otherwise, would give their pursuers a distinct advantage.

Noor was right; if they were to identify the specific mobile tower through which the call from his burner phone had been patched into the main mobile network, picking out their precise location would be a piece of cake. In this forsaken part of the city, his pursuers would have to search not even two dozen properties to get to them. He couldn't call Barkha from here, and he couldn't reach out to Adhiraj or Myra either.

'Here,' Noor said, handing him a basic keypad operated mobile phone. 'It isn't what one could call a technological marvel, but it should serve the purpose for now… And you can use this too if you want,' she added, extending her other hand in which she held the second laptop that Ronit had seen last evening.

'Thank you,' he returned, gracefully accepting both the devices. 'But I guess I won't be able to do much with the laptop either, right? They are probably monitoring all my email ids and social media pages. If I log in to any of of them, they will get to know the IP address for your Wi-Fi connection. So, essentially, I can only use this to surf the internet or play online games,' he added mockingly, looking at the laptop from the corner of his eye.

Noor pulled her shoulders up to express her helplessness.

'Listen, I know this might be a bit too much to ask for, but can you send one of your guys to meet my wife and explain the situation to her? It is really important that she knows I am fine,' Ronit implored.

'We don't have a lot of field operatives functioning in Delhi right now, but I could certainly try,' she said, speaking as she considered his request. 'But that might not be the best idea. If not your government, Zhiming would certainly have her agents watching your house. They might be able to identify my people, putting the entire operation in jeopardy. Only someone having a plausible reason to visit your house should do so, and it can't be anyone who is already under the scanner due to their known proximity to you.'

Ronit plonked himself on the sofa, still holding the phone and laptop in his hands, and began to think. Noor's counsel was accurate, but there had to be a way of establishing contact with Barkha without bringing his known friends into the picture. His situation was strange to say the least, and there weren't many people who would do his bidding without letting their curiosity get in the way. He could visualise his friends inundating him with questions he could not answer and seeking explanations that he could not provide.

The contemplation lasted longer than he had expected, but suddenly he remembered something, and an idea began to take shape in his head.

'Can you make one phone call for me?' he shot out at Noor. She had been busy with her laptop, opting not to interfere with his contemplation.

'To whom?'

'Don't worry, I won't get you to call Barkha,' he returned pertly, excited at having solved the riddle.

'You will have to call my office landline number. If we get lucky, you can straightaway dial the extension number I give you, but if the receptionist picks up, you will have to ask her to connect you with Myra Dhawan. Mind you, the receptionist is our first line of defence against unwanted calls, so you will need to have an airtight introduction ready. Once you get Myra on the line, tell her that you have brought Ghirardelli chocolate squares from Turkey for her… remember, Ghirardelli chocolate squares from Turkey, and say this as soon as she comes on the line. Don't give her an opening to ask you who you are before you have uttered these words. She will know that you are calling on my behalf.'

'Who is this Myra, and can we trust her? You know that your office board line numbers will be under surveillance too, right?' Noor countered.

'Myra works with me. She and Adhiraj are my trusted lieutenants, and they won't let me down. In fact, they would probably be waiting for me to establish contact with them after all this,' he explained.

'These chocolates are Myra's favourite and she had first tasted them when I got her a box on my return from an official trip to Turkey. She fondly remembers that incident till this day and credits me with introducing her to Ghirardelli chocolates. So, as soon as she hears these words, she will know who you are. Myra is trained enough not to say anything that might arouse suspicion on the phone line. To the snoops, the conversation will sound like an ordinary exchange between two friends, nothing more.'

'Okay, and what should I tell her once I have her attention?'

'Ask her to collect the chocolates from *the* coffee shop. Tell her that you are in her part of the town and can reach the coffee shop in twenty minutes or so. And that she should wait for you if she gets there first.'

'And let me guess,' Noor said knowingly, 'we are talking about the Starbucks where we first met.'

'Yes, we are,' Ronit smiled back at her. 'She knows that I am a regular at that particular Starbucks. In fact, both Adhiraj and Myra have accompanied me there several times.'

'The plan is that we will look up the number of the Starbucks outlet on internet and call twenty minutes after you have spoken to her. Even if someone follows her there, which I doubt they will, they won't be able to overhear our conversation. I will have enough time to brief her and set up an under-the-radar communication protocol with her and Adhiraj. This is important, as we might need their help in tracking Zhiming as well,' he elaborated.

'It is a sound plan at the face of it. Let's hope it works. And if it does, one of them can visit your house and meet up with your wife as well. With the goings-on, it won't be out of place for one of your team members to pay a courtesy visit to your house and meet your wife,' she returned.

Ronit did not voice a response. The peculiarity of the situation was making him edgy and nervous. He was seeking help from the woman he had spent the night with to connect with his wife. His position was as embarrassing as it could get. Ronit opted for a meek nod to confirm her assessment of his intentions.

Noor turned out to be a natural at deception. The call was picked up by the overeager receptionist after barely three rings. Her questions were curt—Who are you? What is the purpose of the call?—but Noor was more than ready for her. Maintaining her act of a friend who needed to speak with Myra urgently on a *personal* matter, she was able to overcome the barrier with relative ease. Knowing the receptionist and her ways, Ronit could vouch for the fact that Noor had made the feat look simpler than it really was.

To his respite, the conversation with Myra went exactly as per plan. In fact, Myra paused momentarily when Noor mentioned the chocolates and their country of origin, but the very next moment she jumped into her role with perfection.

'Hey Naisha, when did you return from Turkey? I thought that the honeymoon would give you no time to think about me, but… I love you soooo much… you remembered to bring back chocolates for me. I am so excited… Tell me, when are we meeting? I can't wait to see you,' she shot back excitedly. It was Noor's turn to pause now. She couldn't remember any of her friends back home receiving her phone calls with such enthusiasm. But she was quick to pick up the baton and arrange a meeting as per Ronit's suggestion.

Ronit and Noor spent the next twenty minutes discussing and listing down the topics that needed to be covered in his conversation with Myra. Ronit's plan was playing out perfectly and they needed to make it count.

At the designated time, Noor called up the Starbucks outlet and requested to speak with one of their customers, Myra. The man on the line, without voicing a word of surprise or curiosity, called Myra's name out aloud. Perhaps she had already primed the outlet staff about the impending call. In a few seconds, Noor heard Myra's voice on the line, and she handed over the phone to Ronit.

'Hello, Sir. It is so good to hear your voice finally. We were all so worried,' Myra greeted Ronit, sounding genuinely thrilled to be talking to him.

'Thanks, Myra. I am glad that you were able to decipher my message. You have no idea what it means for me to hear *your* voice today. But first, how private is this conversation? Is there anybody around you who might overhear us?'

'Thankfully they use a cordless phone here. I have carried the handset to my table, and there's no one within an earshot of me. We can talk freely,' she said.

'Great! So, first tell me, what is happening at office? How are people reacting to the news?'

'Oh, everyone knows that this is a cock-and-bull story. All colleagues that I have spoken to believe that the truth will come out soon, but the usual cheer is of course missing from the floor. This morning we had about half a dozen Central Bureau of Investigation (CBI) officers storm into the office. They were being extremely highhanded and started rounding up everyone on our team when Yadav Sir came to our rescue. He gave them quite an earful. He said that this was an elaborate setup to malign RAD and you. He told them that they should go about their investigations, but without letting their enthusiasm make them do something that they might regret later. Listening to him was a delight and it put the officers in their place. Consequently, he made them recede into setting up camp in one of the conference rooms, where they are interviewing people one by one.'

Ronit was pleasantly surprised to learn about Yadav's vocal support for him. The news fueled him with a surge of hope. If Yadav could see through the con, it was probable that his superiors would do so too. Maybe all was not lost just as yet.

'Yadav is right, Myra. I can't reveal much at this point, but this is indeed an elaborate conspiracy by some very powerful enemies of our nation. I came on their radar because I stumbled upon some information that could potentially derail their wicked plans. I still need to figure out some key pieces of the puzzle, but I am hoping to get there soon. This is not a sanctioned RAD operation, so I have limited resources at my disposal. If I am to succeed, I will need all the help that I can get…'

'I am with you, Sir,' she interjected. 'And I can say the same about Adhiraj too. Please let me know what you want us to do, and it will be done.'

'Thank you, Myra. It is very reassuring to hear you say this, but the situation is not so straightforward. As of now I am a fugitive, and anyone who helps me will be committing a criminal offence. The allegations against me might be baseless, but unless I am able to prove my innocence, my situation doesn't really change. In the eyes of people, I will remain a culprit unless I am able to redeem myself by exposing the truth, and no one knows how long that might take. By helping me you will be exposing yourself to great risk, since if this is discovered, it could not only cost you your job but will also make you a delinquent in the eyes of law. The risks of siding with me at this point are way too many…'

'Sir,' she interrupted him, 'you said that this is a plot against our country, and you are in the eye of the storm only because you remained committed to your oath of protecting its honour at all costs. I am sure you could have bailed out, or maybe you still can, and put your own welfare above that of the nation, but you won't do that, just like the soldiers guarding our borders won't fall back at the sight of a threat. You are our idol, Sir, and we have learnt a lot from you, but this decision is not driven by any personal affiliations. I want to stand by you because it is the right thing to do. This is what I have learnt at RAD and from you. If the risks are high, so be it; at least my choice will allow me to live with a clear conscience.'

Myra's words were heart-warming and Ronit struggled to keep their effect from showing in his voice.

'Thank you, Myra. You make me proud,' he said, before hurriedly moving on to the immediate issue at hand. 'So here is what I need you to do. My personal email id has been hacked, and the hackers are probably monitoring it with the hope of discovering my whereabouts in case I log in. My social media profiles would be under their watch too. See if you can find some sort of a thread that could lead us to these hackers. I am as keen to locate them as they are to find me… It might not yield anything in the end, but this is one of the few openings that we have to work with as of now. Put our best guys on the job and let me know if you stumble across anything, no matter how trivial it might appear.'

'A couple of analysts are already working on figuring out if your email id was compromised. In fact, once we got to know from the CBI that the basis for their suspicion was an email that originated from your id, we thought we should arm ourselves with any evidence that we can get to debunk their hypothesis. I will now put more people on the job and get them to look for any live intrusions on other social platforms as well. But the big question is, how do I reach you if I need to?'

'I will give you my burner phone number, memorise it. Just find a clean phone and call me whenever you have anything to share... In fact, between Adhiraj and you, you should speak to me once every few hours anyways. That way I won't need to come up with innovative ways to contact you in case the need arises. If something urgent comes up in the interim, we will find an unconnected phone to place a call on your mobile. You will hear Naisha's voice, and she will make it seem like she has dialled a wrong number. That will be your cue to get to a different phone and call me back on the burner,' Ronit explained. He then vocalised the phone number and checked if Myra had taken note. She had!

'There's another personal help that I need,' Ronit continued. 'I had to leave home in a hurry last evening and I didn't get a chance to explain anything to Barkha. And by now her phone would be tapped and they would be watching the house too... I was hoping if you could pay her a visit and let her know that I am fine...,' he said, allowing his words to tail.

'Of course,' Myra returned. After a brief pause, she added, 'I would have gone to see Ma'am right away, but that might not be the safest course of action for us. We wouldn't want your pursuers to draw any connection between my conversation with Naisha and my visit to your house. That will compromise your ability to contact me through her in the future. Instead, I will pick up a pack of Ghirardelli and head to office. Once there, I will ask Adhiraj to go and visit Ma'am after some time. Don't worry, we will take care of it.'

'Thank you, Myra,' Ronit replied softly.

'You take care of yourself, Sir,' she said, before disconnecting the call.

Chapter 16

Return To Perdition

New Delhi, 7th January 2021

Sunil Bhatia was back to work after a one-day hiatus. Yesterday, he had stayed home on account of an upset stomach, or so he had told everyone in office.

'Bhatia, are you sure you are okay? You can stay home for another couple of days and recuperate if you need to,' his boss had remarked as soon as he set eyes on him.

Bhatia's own eyes were bloodshot, face puffy and yet it looked like he had shrivelled considerably over the past 48 hours. His immensity was still a nightmare for furnituremakers offering replacement warranties on their broken products, but he looked only a fraction of his normally effervescent self today.

'I am perfectly fine, thank you,' he replied. 'I must have eaten something disagreeable to upset my stomach, but I took medicines, and it is alright now... I didn't have fever, cough or any of the other symptoms...'

Spread of the dreaded coronavirus was abating, but the psychosis it had triggered was not. Human ailments, even the commonest of them, were being regarded with utmost suspicion and mistrust. Even a simple sneeze was greeted with such trepidation that even people who were accustomed to relieving themselves in public had become wary of sneezing in front of others.

It was in these trying times that Bhatia's belly had allegedly turned on him. He had returned to work, but his appearance had done precious little to bolster the confidence of his colleagues. His boss's concerned counsel and the explanation he had offered was just the beginning. For the next few hours of the day, he had to offer clarifications and justify his presence in office to so many different people that he was beginning to lose count.

Despite his ordeal, Bhatia found this to be a far more palatable explanation to peddle than the one he had been shielding. The real reason behind his absence from work yesterday and his unsavoury appearance today was such that he could not let it be known to anyone.

In fact, since he had returned home last evening the dreadful flashes of memory had continued to hound him. They had prevented him from getting any sleep at night, and it was on their account that he had decided to turn up for work today. An idle mind, he realised, served as a petri dish for such thoughts. He had hoped to escape them by burying himself under work.

It didn't take long for him to understand that his hope had been misplaced. The ferocity of his trauma was such that he couldn't focus his mind on anything else. He tried to concentrate on work, but it seemed impossible. Whether he was reviewing a draft circular that was due for release or examining a bank exception request, his thoughts would dart back to what was possibly the most harrowing experience of his life.

The evening had started on a promising note. He had arrived at their designated meeting point successfully steering past all the potential hurdles, downed a couple of beers and waited in anticipation. Of course, there was the apprehension that she wouldn't show up, but he kept it under check by leaning on his sanguinity and excitement instead.

His worry turned out to be futile, for she turned up, looking just as ravishing as he had imagined her to be. It was a perfect date, with chit-chat, laughter and the right amount of alcohol to keep their spirits soaring. It was Sonam who had said that she didn't want the evening to end, or something to that effect, and he had simply hurled a bait by proposing that she stay back for the night with him. It was at best a shot in the dark, a man hoping to get lucky in his quest for satisfying his carnal urges. And get lucky, he did.

He managed to find a room at a nearby hotel that wasn't exactly sleazy but didn't believe in meddling in the private affairs of their customers either. Bhatia checked into the room with Sonam, exuding more confidence and familiarity with the situation than he felt. He was on the verge of actualising his fantasy and the last thing he wanted was for her to get edgy and back out at the last minute.

Once they were safely inside the room and he had bolted the door behind him, he let out a sigh of relief. And that was about the time when his fairy tale transformed into a horrific nightmare.

Sunil Bhatia was turning away from the door when he felt a hand grab the neck of his t-shirt and drag him to the bed. His first instinct was that she might be into BDSM, but something about her grip and the fluidity with which she had steered a man of his bulk to precisely where she wanted him, had alarm bells going off in his head.

'So, you like to dominate?' he asked her casually, starting up from where she had flung him on the bed.

'Shut up, you bastard!' she shot out ferociously. It seemed as if a furball had suddenly transformed into a menacing being that he no longer recognised. She was certainly not the demure Sonam who had walked into the room with him. Her eyes were stone-cold, and he could see her jaws tremble intimidatingly with the clenching of her teeth.

'Have you ever seen yourself in the mirror? You really thought that I was going to sleep with you?' she continued, not making any attempts to shield her disgust. 'I am going to fuck you alright, but not how you might have been expecting.'

'But... But what happened? What have I done?' he was barely able to mutter.

Her reply was a hard smack across his face. The impact was such that it made the alcohol in his body evaporate instantly. He was startled and he could see stars, but most of all he was petrified to the core.

'Take off your clothes and turn on your belly,' she commanded.

Sunil obeyed without offering any resistance. Something told him that despite his size, he was in no position to take her on. She could overpower him at will. His pulsating cheek put to rest any ideas of engaging her in a dialogue that he might have considered.

'That too,' she said, pointing at the only remaining piece of clothing shielding his dignity—his briefs. She had pulled out her own belt and it was hanging in her hand like a deadly whip.

'Now,' she screamed, snapping the belt, and letting it land somewhere between his buttocks and inner thighs. Bhatia had to bite his tongue and yet a muffled shriek escaped his lips.

She then pulled his hands behind his back and tied them with the belt. The efficiency of her moves reminded Sunil of his mother's proficiency when she worked in the kitchen. It was a strange comparison alright, but Sonam seemed as trained in what she was doing as his mother was in her culinary arts. Next, she claimed his belt from the loops of his denim and wound his ankles together with it. Sunil Bhatia was now officially her captive. He couldn't see what she was doing, and he couldn't fathom what was happening to him, so he buried his face deeper into the stained bedsheet and began to weep.

It was a long time after that he heard the next sound. It was a knock on the door. He was half frightened and half alert. It was odd for the hotel staff to knock on rooms at this hour, unless there was a situation that required them to do so. He was praying that it was the police conducting a surprise raid on the premises. The situation he was in would land him in a soup, no doubt, but nothing he couldn't manage by greasing a few palms. At least he would be rescued from whatever it was that the girl was planning to do.

The streak of optimism didn't last long though. Sunil heard the creak of the bolt being drawn back, followed by light whispers in an unfamiliar tongue. Then he heard someone step inside the room, one or maybe two people, before the door was locked again. It clearly wasn't the police. She had probably summoned her accomplices and they were now ready to do whatever they meant to do to him. Sunil Bhatia was trembling with fear, letting out a strange cooing sound, quite like the low-pitched moans of a terribly hungry puppy.

'I am going to untie your hands now. But remember, you twitch a muscle without being asked to do so and you will wish that you were never born,' she warned him. Immediately thereafter, his hands were unfastened and spread out beside him on the bed. He felt his shoulders collapse with relief, but he made no attempts to move his hands.

He felt a palm land on his back, and with its support someone straddled him; like a masseuse about to relieve him of his pain. As he felt the warm body against his own, a sudden realisation made the hair at the nape of his neck rise. The intruder was a man, and stark naked, quite like his own self. Sunil could feel his manhood against him, as if someone had placed a tightly rolled hot towel in the burrow of his lower back. He wiggled and tried to shout, but Sonam was on him in an instant.

Grabbing a fistful of hair, she pulled his head up and said, 'Not a sound… If you want to live, I don't want to hear a single sound coming from here.' For effect, she touched the tip of the knife she held in her other hand to his lips. The message was delivered and adequately received.

The next few minutes were registered in his memory like a blinding flash of bright light. Sunil experienced a tearing pain unlike anything he had ever encountered before. It was as if somebody had mercilessly drilled a hole into him. The vigour of the pain was such that it transported him to a different paradigm altogether. It seemed as if he had been pulled out of his body into a place where he could see nothing but a burst of luminescence. He was still connected with his mortal body, hearing and feeling things, but only in infrequent spurts.

Sunil could feel that the pain had acquired a teasing rhythm of its own, and he could hear feet shuffling around him, but he could see nothing. Then he felt a damp cloth press against his nose and mouth, a strange citric smell followed, and the light around him started to dim. He felt his sensory functions weakening, until all his senses had summarily dissolved into complete blackness. Sunil Bhatia's ordeal was over for the time being.

When he opened his eyes next, the bring light of a new day was streaming in from the gap between the curtains. He propped himself on the bed and glanced around. He was on the same bed in the hotel room, still stark naked. A bundle of clothing on the floor caught his eye and he was relieved that his assailants had decided to leave them behind. His head was heavy, and he could feel his intestines contracting with hunger, but he had bigger issues that needed to be tackled first.

Sunil glanced at the bedside table, hoping to find his watch. But he immediately realised that the watch was still wrapped around his wrist. He had never had the time to take it off as he usually did before he went to bed. He checked the time—3.30 pm. He had remained unconscious for anywhere between twelve and fourteen hours.

Suddenly he remembered something and looked back at the table. There it was a bundle of photographs kept neatly on his bedside. He had seen it while looking for his watch, but it hadn't quite registered. And now when he realised what it was, he was struck by a stab of nervous trepidation.

He reached out for the bundle but winced and retracted his extended hand abruptly. A sharp pain in his anal region had forced him to withdraw. Gritting his teeth, he reached cautiously for the pictures once again. The pain proved far more bearable with the controlled movement, and he succeeded in claiming them. As soon as he saw the first picture of the stack, he felt his heart pause midbeat. He saw the next one and the one after that, and his jaw continued to drop with each photograph.

They were photos of Sunil Bhatia being sodomised by a masked man. There were closeups and long shots, but each one of them deftly clicked to make it look like a consensual liaison. None of the pictures had captured his tied feet or anything else that might have hinted at coercion or rape. To an onlooker, the pictures would seem nothing more than artistic captures of the most intimate moments between two lovers. He let the pictures drop in his lap and clutched his head between his hands. Sunil Bhatia didn't know what the girl wanted from him, but in one night she had seized control of his whole life. She could do with him what she pleased. If she asked him to jump out the window, he would have no option but to abide.

Sunil remained holding his position for a long time, thinking about all the things he could have done differently to avoid the situation he had landed himself in. He cursed himself, pledged that he wouldn't look lustily at another girl for the rest of his wretched life, and he thought about what Sonam, or whatever her real name was, might want from him. He was a middle-class salaried man with hardly any noteworthy savings or assets. He would be good for a few thousand rupees, a couple of lakhs if he stretched, but definitely not more. Why would they go to such lengths to trap him for that kind of money?

It seemed implausible, but the fact remained that it was him that they had trapped and not someone richer. He must have been an easy target, a lamb who had required little goading to stomp its way to the sacrificial altar. All he could do now was wait and hope that they kept his financial standing in mind while framing their demands.

It was evening by the time a comatose Sunil Bhatia had managed to return home. The sight of him had prompted his concerned wife to strike conversation, but he had snarled back at her and retreated into the bedroom. His wife, guided by her own assessment of the situation, had served his dinner in the room and parked herself on the couch for the night. Sunil had not stepped out of the room until today morning.

Liberal applications of moisturiser had helped Sunil check his physical trauma, but the mental agony was quite another thing.

He had been defiled and scarred, and the wounds were far from healing. He had hoped that work would help him divert his mind, but it had failed miserably. Till lunch time, despite his best efforts, he had managed to get only a fraction of his usual work done. He was staring at the screen, trying to make sense of the words stitched together in the open Word document, when he was interrupted by the alert of an incoming text message.

'Please come to Soul Café in Paharganj at 6 pm today. I will be waiting,' the message read.

The sender's number was not saved on his phone and neither had they bothered to reveal their identity, but Bhatia had a fair idea about who it was. The blackmailers were ready to make their demands, and he had no option but to do their bidding.

'Who is this?' he replied, nevertheless.

'This is your photographer. Be there or I will be forced to share my masterpieces with the rest of the world.'

He read the message pensively and returned the phone on his desk. The Word document on his screen would have to wait for some time before it could reclaim his attention.

After a brief pause, he picked up his phone and typed another reply: I will be there!

Chapter 17

A Shot In The Dark

New Delhi, 7th January 2021

'It can't be the vaccination programme that she is after, and it probably isn't the farmers' protest either,' Noor stated pensively. 'We need to think afresh. What are the other big vulnerabilities your country is facing right now? Operation Bamboo Garden is a tool for Chinese economic annexation. They create conditions where target nations are compelled to accept Chinese aid or investments despite the obnoxious terms that accompany them. We need to look for weaknesses which have the potential to bring the Indian economy to such a brink. That is where Zhiming will be looking to strike.'

Ronit let out a deep sigh and lifted his hands in exasperation. 'It could be anything… From targeting one of our nuclear facilities to instigating communal discord, there are endless avenues that she could choose from to deal a significant blow to the economy… This pandemic has achieved what the Chinese misadventures on the northern frontiers could not. Today, our unemployment numbers are at an all-time high, inflation is peaking and our forex reserves are depleting rapidly. At this juncture, even a relatively mild trigger would have an amplified effect on eroding global confidence in the Indian economy.'

Noor was listening to him restlessly.

After establishing contact with Myra, they had buried themselves in trying to ascertain Zhiming's whereabouts. Noor believed that her countermove against Ronit meant that Zhiming's plan was close to being set in motion. 'Else, why would she strike back so vehemently? It was a simple search you had triggered. She could have chosen to lie low and wait for the heat to settle. Or, she could have adopted a more subtle approach and tried to find out how much you know about their plans and what your source is. The fact that she went with an unhinged frontal assault could only mean that she is ready to execute whatever she has been working on. If I had to hazard a guess, I'd say that she is within days of dealing her blow,' Noor reasoned.

They got down to scanning news articles with the hope of encountering something that could point them in the direction of a likely target. Zhiming was a ghost, and with RAD's resources no longer in play, they didn't know where to begin their search.

'The only other notable thing I can think of is the farmer's agitation. Farmer groups camping on the outskirts of Delhi are seeking permission to march into the city on Republic Day. Although 26 January is still nearly three weeks away, the parade could be on her radar. The Republic Day parade is a global event and any untoward incident there will instantly be magnified by global media. And if the disruption were to be caused by our own protesting farmers, we will undoubtedly become the laughing stock of the world,' Ronit had proposed.

Noor had her reservations. She believed that with the Chinese funding of the protests having become a subject of television debates, it no longer remained a probable target for Zhiming. 'It can be one of the many strikes, but it can't be her knockout punch,' she had argued. 'Moreover, anything that the farmers do will bring their own cause into limelight. It will force the government to repeal the controversial laws, or if they get swayed and do anything to offend India's sovereignty, they will become the anti-heroes and lose their base of sympathisers. I don't see how either of these eventualities could serve the Chinese.'

They debated the efficacy of looking for Zhiming's trail around the arena of the farmers' protest and in the vicinity of its leaders. In the end, it was the lack of alternatives that shaped their decision. They had nowhere else to look, and this was as good a place as any to begin their search for the elusive Chinese operative.

Noor remained glued to her phone, shouting instructions and seeking updates from members of her own network for several hours before sharing her findings with Ronit. Her people had scanned footages, reached out to sources close to those leading the protests and checked for signs of manipulation in the narrative about the issue playing out in cyberspace. They had found nothing remotely Chinese anywhere.

'We had cultivated some vital assets within the inner circles of the protesting groups after we discovered that Chinese money was flowing into it. But that was initially. It appears that after your agencies cracked down on their conduits, the Chinese have washed their hands off the agitation completely. Some propagandists and unscrupulous groups are trying to instigate the protestors, but that it purely for their own selfish motives. None of them have any known affiliations with the Chinese or with Zhiming,' she had explained.

Ronit was in a precarious position. His entire life hinged on finding this one elusive person, and they were just as close to their goal as they had been when they began their search. He had just explained to Noor how the Indian economy was battered with the multiple blows it had endured in the recent past, and how Zhiming could pick and choose her triggers for sending it on a further downward spiral.

'We can't be shooting in the dark anymore; we don't have that kind of time,' Ronit persisted. 'We have no way of ascertaining whether any target that we shortlist is indeed the one that she's going after. Like this, we will keep hopping from one wild goose chase to another, while she concludes her mission and goes back home. If we are to find her, we will have to get back to looking for Zhiming the person. We know what she looks like, and we know that she is likely to be somewhere in Delhi right now. Our best bet of finding her is to follow the threads of the information that we possess.'

'You are right, that would be ideal. If fact, that is exactly the thought that had prompted me to seek your help. But now, in the absence of RAD's means and machinations, how do you suppose we go about finding Zhiming in this city of nearly twenty million people?'

Ronit considered her words, as if savouring them in his mouth before ingesting them, and then his face lit up all of a sudden. 'I think I might know someone who can help us, but we will have to go to him. Is it safe for us to step out of this place?'

'Yes, as long as we exercise caution and do nothing to invite unnecessary attention upon us, we should be safe. Where are we heading though?' Noor queried.

'Noida. It is one of the satellite cities in the National Capital Region.'

'I know, Noida,' she said, her brows coming together suddenly. 'But wouldn't we have to cross a toll booth to get there? The toll plaza cameras are positioned to capture the insides of each passing vehicles. We will run the risk of getting photographed.'

'Don't worry, the toll road is just one among the many entry points into Noida. We will not have to cross the booth if we don't intend to,' Ronit returned. Oddly, he felt good telling her something she didn't already know, no matter how trivial the slice of information happened to be.

It was early evening already, and Noor suggested that they grab a bite before leaving. She offered to whip up some instant noodles and headed into the kitchen.

She had barely left when a loud ring startled Ronit. It was his burner phone announcing an incoming call from an unknown landline number. The unusually shrill ringtone was going to take some getting used to. Ronit received the call and warily pressed the instrument against his ear.

'Hi, it's me,' he heard Adhiraj's unmistakable voice on the line. 'Just wanted to let you know that I met her and passed on your message. She asked you to focus on whatever you have to do without worrying about anything else.'

'Thank you,' he said, relieved to learn that Barkha was no longer in the dark about his present situation. The tacit support that she had relayed through Adhiraj held more meaning for him than he had ever anticipated. It had fuelled him with a sudden surge of hope and optimism. 'Listen,' he added, 'call me on the same number in a couple of hours if you can. If I am lucky, I might need your help with something.'

Adhiraj acknowledged the request and disconnected the call. The thought of Barkha had made Ronit curious about the way the entire matter was being presented to the general public. He was keen to know if his name had been revealed as a possible suspect and the extent to which it had been sullied already. He reached out for the laptop and opened the web browser.

Under different circumstances he would have simply searched for his name in recently published news articles, but in the current situation that would be akin to sending smoke signals to draw attention of his pursuers. They were bound to be monitoring all online search requests for certain keywords, his name being an obvious inclusion to the list, and it would be easy for them to zero in on the origin of such a request.

So, Ronit had to manually hunt for relevant stories in digital editions of newspapers. He scanned through the first and then the second newspaper, and to his dismay, came up with nothing. Two of the country's leading dailies had not carried the story for some reason. He typed the name of the news portal which had first broken the story in the browser and scrolled through the recent posts. The article from the previous evening was still there, but there were no follow-up stories or updates thereafter.

'This is strange,' he said, looking up at Noor who had just emerged holding two plates full of steaming noodles. 'The story of the information leak has not been picked by any of the major media outlets. Apart from the article from yesterday, I haven't found another mention of the incident anywhere.'

'That's good for us, isn't it? You can at least eat in peace now,' Noor returned with a smile. Once she had settled on the couch, she continued, 'This isn't all that surprising actually! Your government will be wary of anything that could turn people against the vaccination programme. News of this leak will not breed vaccine hesitancy directly, but who knows how the opposition might twist the story. It is highly likely that the authorities have used their muscle to bury the news. And there is no reason for Zhiming to push it back in circulation either. With you under investigation, her purpose has been accomplished anyway.'

This was the second positive thing that Ronit had heard within a very short span. Perhaps the tide was starting to turn.

It didn't take long for them to finish their meal, and they were soon racing down the arterial road which would lead them back to humanity. Ronit was wearing a pair of sunglasses, a mask and the same cap that he had worn last evening, all accessories prescribed by Noor as precautionary measures. He held the steering wheel this time while Noor sat alongside him.

'There are more male drivers on Delhi roads than females. A vehicle driven by a woman will register easily in the minds of onlookers and they might recollect more than they should if they were to be questioned later. It is better that you drive,' she had clarified, noticing his hesitation. Ronit had always driven a hatchback, never a sedan. He was skeptical of his ability to handle the car's size, an excuse too trite to express in wake of Noor's elucidation.

Ronit's concern proved to be unfounded though. He was steering the vehicle like an expert by the time they emerged on the main road and coalesced with the early evening traffic.

The vehicular presence on the roads seemed to have returned to the pre-pandemic era. Cars jostling to get to their destinations, honking and swerving drivers, and passengers buried in their smartphone screens—it was as if the city had healed itself and decided to move on.

Ronit wondered if this was a display of courage or idiocy. With epidemiologists screaming for people not to let their guard down, the defiance and bravado he was witnessing around him could prove to be a recipe for disaster.

And he wondered if he too would emerge from his own catastrophe with similar elan and poise. The signs were not very encouraging thus far. Despite Noor's assurances of safety, he couldn't help but look at every driver he passed and each pedestrian who caught his eye with unease and suspicion.

He was like a gullible prey in a dense murderous forest, scared of the slightest movement he saw or hustle he heard. This was not a life he was prepared for. This was not a life he could ever get used to leading.

Chapter 18

An Odd Ally

Noida, 7th January 2021

'5:18' was the time displayed on the car's digital dashboard when Ronit turned off the engine. They had arrived at their destination—a small, standalone house in a busy part of Noida, not far from the Delhi border.

The street was lined with similar matchbox style structures on both sides, some with their outer rooms converted into unauthorised shops displaying everything from bright plastic toys to duplicate apparels proudly exhibiting distorted insignia of high-street fashion brands. They could see a few vegetable and food carts, nothing fancy, only small commercial enterprises to make ends meet. A few cars and two-wheelers were parked on the sides, leaving just enough space for a medium-sized vehicle to pass through. Ronit had parallel parked the Verna in a vacant spot between a taxi and an autorickshaw.

As they climbed out of the car, the familiar stench of a neglected middle class neighborhood collided against their nostrils—a dank cocktail of burning spices, decomposing garbage, human sweat and unchecked vehicular emissions. This part of the city had probably come up when the real estate prices in Noida were still favourable for realising the middle class dream of owning a house. Since then, the city had progressed leaps and bounds, leaving the early settlers with astronomically priced properties that had no takers.

Ronit walked a few paces, with Noor close on his heels, and stopped in front of a painted metal gate. 'Sharma, House Number: 117,' was engraved on a marble plate affixed next to the entrance. He pressed the call bell and heard the notes of a popular *Arti* tune play out in the distance. Shortly after, the gate was opened, and a middle-aged man peered out at them.

His gaze paused momentarily on Ronit's face before a flicker of recognition appeared in his eyes. 'Sir, you?' he said, nervously looking at him and Noor. 'Has he done something again?'

'No, Mr Sharma, he has done nothing wrong. You have an exceptionally gifted son, and you should be proud of him,' Ronit replied in the friendliest tone he could muster. 'In fact, we were hoping to see Lovlesh on a project where we could use his help. Can we come in?'

Rakesh Sharma stepped aside hurriedly, making way for them to step inside. 'I know he is good with computers, but sometimes I worry about him. At this age he should be going out, making friends, but he chooses to remain holed up in his room all the time,' he said, sounding every bit the worried parent that he was, as he led them into the living room.

It was a modest space with all the usual furnishings—a wooden sofa set, a television, a four-seater dining table and a wall-mounted air conditioner. A large wooden cabinet covering the majority of the left wall was the star attraction of the room. It displayed dozens of trophies, plaques and framed certificates—the cumulative earnings of the proud Sharma family.

'Sir, Madam, please take a seat,' he said, pointing at the sofa. 'Anju, will you get us some tea and biscuits please?' he hollered instructions to his wife, who was probably in the kitchen already.

'No, we won't have anything,' Ronit protested. 'It will be nice if you can take us to Lovlesh's room instead. The matter that we need to consult him on is slightly time-sensitive…'

Rakesh objected vehemently. It was unthinkable for him to let his guests leave the house without having anything, and that too when one of the visitors happened to be a senior government official who had saved his son from certain doom. It was only when Ronit accepted his offer of having the tea served in Lovlesh's room that Rakesh Sharma led them back to the stairway they had seen near the entrance. He took the flight of stairs and stopped before the door of the single rooftop room.

It was a rectangular structure with plain brick walls that seemed to have been placed on top of the house as an afterthought. Ronit could hear a soft drone emanating from within the room.

'This is where he spends all of his waking hours. I will knock and let him know that you are here,' he said, depositing a series of thuds with his open palm on the door. 'He doesn't appreciate any of us entering his room. Even his mother has to align the schedule for the weekly cleaning with him in advance.'

'Lovlesh, open up,' he shouted, after the banging went unanswered. 'Biswas Sir and Madam from RAD are here to see you.' Ronit didn't bother to correct the introduction of Noor he had offered. It would have been difficult to explain to Mr Rakesh Sharma, the teacher, that the seemingly harmless woman he was about to let into his son's den was an international agent capable of ending human lives with her bare hands.

The mention of Ronit's name had an immediate effect. Like the magical phrase used to open the mouth of the cave in the story of *Ali Baba and the Forty Thieves*, within moments of its utterance the door to the room flew open. 'Hello, Sir. This is such a nice surprise. Please come in,' an excited Lovlesh emerged from it to greet them.

'I will come back with the tea,' Rakesh Sharma said before receding down the steps. He was clearly not welcome in Lovlesh's den.

As soon as he stepped inside the room, Ronit felt the temperature around him drop considerably. Lovlesh had the air conditioner running full blast on an early-January evening in northern India. He saw Noor grit her teeth to deal with the cold. The room, with its red and black theme, was like an oasis of modernity amid the expanse of middle class traditionality. It was adorned by a faux leather couch, a small refrigerator and randomly strewn magazines, empty Coca-Cola cans and chips packets. At the farther end was a La-Z-Boy recliner facing a desk with two large computer screens.

'What on earth! Where did you get all this from?' Ronit couldn't help but exclaim once he made sense of the hardware he was looking at. In this little room, Lovlesh had enough processing power to put any medium-sized data processing outfit to shame. The entire set up would have cost several million rupees, and some of the gadgetry he could see was not even available in the open market yet. It was quite a shock to find the boy amid such luxuries when his family appeared to be living in relative austerity around him.

'This equipment is necessary for what I do. I have procured everything from my own hard-earned money,' Lovlesh replied defensively.

'Your own money! How do you make the kind of money that allows you to afford all this? Are your parents even aware of the amount this must have cost?'

'I have made my money by mining bitcoins, participating in ethical hackathons and other harmless contests on the dark web. I swear, I haven't been doing anything illegal. In fact, since we last met, I haven't even surfed the dark web,' he explained anxiously. 'Initially we could mine bitcoins using ordinary computers, and I tasted some early successes with the basic system I had. Then, I invested my earnings to buy the ASIC hardware which is specially designed for mining bitcoins… You know that if I don't keep my equipment updated, I will turn obsolete within a matter of days. And my father would understand none of it, so I had no option but to keep him in the dark.'

The boy's explanation made sense. Priced at over Rs. 2 million apiece, bitcoins were indeed capable of funding the entire setup. The disappointment in his father's eyes had perhaps acted as a barrier for Lovlesh to open up to his parents. He was still a child after all, and his inability to predict his father's reactions was a likely enough trigger for him to recede into his shell. He was aware of several instances where children had kept their most treasured achievements concealed for the fear of facing rejection at the hands of their loved ones.

'You think this equipment will be sufficient to get our work done?' Noor asked Ronit. It was a rhetorical question meant to bring his focus back on the task at hand, and it landed precisely where it was meant to. Ronit realised that he was deviating from the very purpose that had brought him to Lovlesh's doorstep.

'Any equipment is only as good as the person using it. I know that Lovlesh is good at what he does, but whether he is good enough to do the job, only he can tell,' Ronit replied to Noor, before turning to face the boy. 'We have come to seek your help in locating someone who might be anywhere in the city right now. All we have on this person is a couple of photographs, and we must find her without hacking into any government or public databases. It is vital that we track her soon as several lives might depend on it. Tell me, Lovlesh, can you think of some way to locate this woman for us? I am fine even it requires the rules to be bent a little.'

Lovlesh, after listening intently to the request, slumped down on the recliner and fixed his eyes on one corner of the ceiling. 'Photographs... but we will need to match them with something... If not with the known records, then what can we match them with...,' he was murmuring to himself, when a knock sounded on the door.

'Lovlesh, I am leaving the tea at the door. Take it inside before it gets cold,' Rakesh Sharma's curt words followed. Lovlesh did not offer an oral response. Instead, he waited for the footsteps to recede before making for the door. If the interaction was anything to go by, the father–son relationship was in definite need for some mending.

When Lovlesh returned with the tray, there was an unmistakable spark in his eyes. 'There is one thing we could try. It might not be a foolproof method, but if we get lucky it can produce results almost instantaneously,' he said as he handed them their cups.

'What is it?' Ronit and Noor shot out simultaneously.

Lovlesh returned to the recliner and began to explain. 'Millions of photographs are clicked and uploaded by people of Delhi on various social media platforms each day. In the background of these pictures, you will find unsuspecting victims who get captured without even being aware that they are in the line of the camera's vision. The daily count of such unwitting subjects whose pictures find their way into cyberspace is in multiples of the number of actual pictures uploaded. If you have a reasonably active and mobile life, there is a high probability that you will feature in at least one such photograph every week.'

'Go on,' Ronit said, when Lovlesh paused to check if he still had their attention. The revelation was shocking but logical, and Ronit was curious about where the boy was heading with it.

'The bandwidth needed to run a facial match program of such proportions makes it impossible for any single agency to comb the entire collection of data. However, the repository becomes far more useful if the search is carried out by hundreds of different crawler programs sitting on different servers across the world.'

'But how will we activate these hundreds of programs you are talking about?' Ronit queried. He was completely absorbed by Lovlesh's oratory, quite unlike Noor. She seemed to have given up on trying to decipher the technicalities. She was studying the graffiti on the walls, having left the deliberations to the experts.

'By posting a contest on the dark web!' Lovlesh responded. 'There are thousands of cryptocurrency miners working day and night to mine bitcoins. If we offer bitcoins as reward for those who can find a match for your picture on the internet, there is no reason why a majority of them wouldn't want to try their luck. The task is no different than trying to mine bitcoins; if anything, it is only simpler.'

'How safe is this method? What if a powerful enemy

who doesn't want her to be discovered is watching the dark web?' Noor said, slipping into the conversation suddenly.

'Oh, the dark web is totally safe. The bulletins have restricted access and only those with verified credentials can see the posts. Moreover, even if your enemies were to chance upon the contest, all they will know is that it's a race to find a match for a picture. The picture won't obviously be posted upfront. It will be an inconspicuous post, and they will have no reason whatsoever to delve into the specific picture for which a match is being sought. And if that is not enough, there is no way for anyone to detect the real person behind a dark web identity. As I said, this is totally safe,' Lovlesh decoded the problem for her passionately.

'Plus, they already know that we are looking for her and that we have her photograph in our possession. So, in any case it won't change the status quo,' Ronit added. 'How many bitcoins will we need to make this work?' he asked Lovlesh next.

'Three coins in all should be a safe number. We can pledge a bitcoin each for the three most recent matches, which should offer a good enough probability to get them hooked.'

'Three bitcoins!' Ronit exclaimed. 'That will cost over $1 million!'

'Don't worry about that... Just post the contest,' Noor interjected, addressing Lovlesh to begin with. 'The reward will be payable only when the participants are successful in locating her. A million dollars is nothing if it helps us get to her. Trust me! I will find the money,' she added for Ronit's benefit.

Lovlesh was ecstatic to get the go-ahead. This was like a dream come true for him. He was working for a senior official from India's premier intelligence agency, and his idea had just received a backing of a million dollars. He was feeling more purposeful now than he had ever felt in his life. While he got down to playing with his keyboard, Ronit and Noor stepped out onto the terrace.

Despite the uncertainty and distress, the sight of the setting sun was soothing for the soul. They sipped their tea in silence, staring at the marvellous hues of nature.

In just over half an hour, a beaming Lovlesh emerged from the room. 'We have got two hits already,' he shared excitedly. Ronit and Noor rushed back into the den behind him with a sudden spring in their strides.

'This is from yesterday morning, from the Rajiv Chowk metro station,' he said, expanding a small photograph to cover the screen. It was a selfie of two girls, college students perhaps, with the metro train in the background. Other passengers could be seen on the platform behind them. 'Here, this is our girl,' Lovlesh said, pointing at a half-turned female face that had been accidentally captured in the picture.

The girl in question was wearing black tights and a denim jacket. She had Mongoloid features alright, but with only a part of her face in view, it was difficult to draw conclusions. She was walking away from the tracks, towards the exit. Ronit turned to look at Noor, seeking a confirmation of her identity.

She bent forward to take a closer look and shook her head sideways. 'Wait,' she suddenly said, 'this man, can we enlarge the image and look at him?'

Lovlesh followed the instructions and enlarged the image of a man who was walking in the same direction as the girl, only about half a dozen steps behind. He was short and stocky, and unmistakably Chinese. His full face was visible in the picture too.

'Get a print of his face,' Noor said, pointing at the man. 'If this is indeed her, she won't be travelling alone in the Metro at a crucial stage of her mission. She will have agents watching her at a distance for her protection. He must be one of them… And what was the second hit you mentioned?'

Lovlesh gave the print command before putting up a second picture. This one showed a group of friends making merry in a bar. Behind their table, in the far corner, a man and a woman could be seen sitting across each other, looking at each other over the beer pints separating them.

'That's her,' Noor said excitedly. 'But who's the man she is with?'

It was Ronit's turn to view the picture closely now. 'He looks like any average working-class Indian man. If he's not one of those clandestine operatives from your trade, it shouldn't be difficult to figure out his identity.' Turning towards Lovlesh, he asked, 'When and where was this one clicked?'

'This is from the day before, in the evening, at a bar in Sector 29, Gurugram.'

'Perfect! Look at the camera feeds from the entry points to the market or the parking lots to see how he arrived. If it was a private car, the registration number will tell you who he is. And if he came in a cab, you could get into the cab company's booking systems and figure out his identity,' Ronit advised.

'But that would mean hacking into one or more public servers,' Lovlesh said, pulling his brows up. It was the look for a child eager to indulge in the extra TV time he had been given, but not before he pointed out the inconsistencies in his parents' stance on the matter.

'You can't run a match for the girl's pictures anywhere—that's the only rule—other than that everything is fair game,' Ronit said, not caring for the wry smile appearing on Lovlesh's face.

'Wait, it seems we have another match,' Lovlesh said, turning his attention towards the screen as soon as the machine let out a ping. 'This was just about an hour back, in Paharganj,' he added, as he pulled up the image on the screen. He then read out the description mentioned at the bottom of the photograph, 'the picture was clicked and uploaded by an Israeli backpacker. It is from Soul Café in Paharganj, clicked at 6.08 pm today.'

'She's with the same man,' Ronit said, as he identified their target in the background. Noor peered over his shoulders and said, 'how long will it take for us to get there?'

'At this hour, about forty-five minutes would be my guess.'

'Let's get going then,' she said to Ronit.

Looking at Lovlesh, she added, 'give me your cryptocurrency wallet details. I will have the bitcoins wired within the hour… Keep working on identifying this man and call us on this number as soon as you have anything. I have a feeling that he is going to be a crucial cog in the entire story.'

'Thank you, Lovlesh! What you have achieved today is nothing short of a miracle. We will sit and chat about it at length someday, but till then remember that your country owes you one,' Ronit said, ruffling the hair on the boy's head, as they exited his den.

Lovlesh looked at them depart, revelling in the words of praise he had just heard. No one around him even understood his work, let alone appreciate it. And coming from Ronit Biswas, each word was like a priceless medal for him.

Chapter 19

Scent Of The Enemy

New Delhi, 7th January 2021

It was 7.50 pm by the time their car rolled out of Lovlesh's lane. The traffic on the roads was sparse, and after many years, Ronit noticed traces of fog in the evening air. The forced clampdown on human activity had allowed mother nature the freedom to reclaim some of her lost glory. Like the proverbial glass, the dreadful pandemic had its half-full side too.

They had not even exited Noida to enter Delhi when Noor's phone buzzed. She received the call and switched on the speaker for Ronit's benefit.

'The man's name is Sunil Bhatia. He lives in Minto Road with his wife and son. I will text you his complete address and phone number,' Lovlesh's voice rang within the confines of the car. 'He drives an old model Zen and spends most of his time at office or at home. He doesn't have much of a social life...'

'Lovlesh, skip the biographical sketch and stick to the relevant pieces, please. What does this Bhatia do? Where does he work?' Ronit said, interrupting Lovlesh's oratory.

'I was getting to that… Sunil Bhatia is a General Manager with the Reserve Bank of India. He heads the RTGS platform for northern India…'

His words hit them like a sledgehammer. Ronit and Noor exchanged a glance and instantly they knew that the picture emerging in their minds was quite similar. Ronit thanked Lovlesh and asked him to remain on standby for any urgent help that they might require.

'Her target is the RTGS platform,' Noor broke the momentary silence that followed Lovlesh's call.

'The Real Time Gross Settlement system is the backbone of the Indian economy. Most corporations and individuals use this platform to carry out high value fund transfers. If she succeeds in planting a bug in the RTGS system, it will send the entire economy into a tizzy. A bug can potentially clean up all the bank accounts from which an RTGS transaction is initiated; and we are talking about several million savings and current accounts here. This could lead to complete collapse of the country's banking system,' Ronit said, articulating the enormity of the threat that Zhiming posed.

'Not to mention that it will trigger immediate retraction of funds by the Foreign Institutional Investors, and your central bank will not have adequate foreign exchange reserves to return their money. Your policy makers will have to choose between the near-impossible task of raising capital from somewhere or watch their country being declared a bankrupt nation. At such a juncture, if the Chinese were to propose a bailout package, your government will be in no position to turn them down. You will have to accept all their terms, irrespective of the repercussions they might have in the future,' Noor added, painting an even bleaker image of what Zhiming's success could imply. Her words melted into a weighty silence.

It was Ronit who punctured the quiet with his words. 'We can't let her succeed. We have to stop her, no matter what it takes,' he said fervently. 'Do you think they will still be at the café when we get there?'

'Honestly, I don't think so! Zhiming wouldn't want to spend even a minute more than what is necessary in such an exposed setting. But if we look carefully, we might pick up some vital clues for sure...' Noor was still speaking when Ronit's ringing phone interrupted her. He picked up the call, switched on the speaker and waited quietly till he heard Adhiraj's voice on the line.

'The number I am calling from is clean. You can reach me on this anytime. It is actually a friend's old phone number, which he doesn't use much now. I have borrowed it from him for a couple of days,' he said.

'That's great! And you couldn't have called at a better time,' Ronit replied. 'There is something I need your help with. I will send you the address and phone number of a man,' he added, explaining how Sunil Bhatia had been in contact with the Chinese agent, Zhiming, and what he suspected her ulterior motives to be. 'We need to get to her somehow, and this Bhatia is our only key. Find out what you can about his whereabouts, or anything else that might lead us to his Chinese friend. There is a high possibility that she has trapped him into helping her. So, look for any patterns in how they came in contact as well as the mediums and frequency of their contact. There's bound to be something there that can lead us to her.'

'I will do that! I hope there's no risk if I use my work laptop and credentials to investigate though? I mean, if we need answers in quick time, we might need to bend our fingers a little,' Adhiraj enquired.

'Bhatia might not be particularly threatening, but the Chinese lady certainly is. In fact, all this began when I set up a search to match her picture against some of the databases using my credentials. So, while you can leverage the RAD resources, I will strongly recommend against actions that might trigger any preset alarms. Using traceable searches with names or pictures is definitely not advised. Stick to relatively covert means like accessing the phone company records or mobile number tracking. Rely on manual channels to the extent possible.'

Having warned Adhiraj of the likely threats, he handed the phone to Noor and asked her to send Zhiming's pictures and Sunil Bhatia's particulars to the number that Adhiraj had called from. They had entered the Connaught Place outer circle already and were to arrive at their destination in a few minutes.

Soul Café turned out to be a watering hole hidden in the labyrinthian bylanes of Paharganj. Despite the navigation aid to guide them, they found themselves going round in circles, until they decided to park the car and embark on the hunt afoot.

It was a little past eight and yet the lane they stepped inside, with most shops lining it having downed their shutters, looked deserted. A little ahead, they could see some signs of human presence. Coloured light spilling across the street and the rhythmic tempo of trance music emanating from an open door acted as guiding beacons for the duo. As they stepped forward, keeping a cautious eye for any of Zhiming's associates who might be lurking in the alley, Ronit received a message alert on his phone.

It was Adhiraj. 'Our man is off the grid. His number is switched off and his wife doesn't know where he is. I spoke with her on the house landline number. She seemed worried about him too; said that he wasn't feeling well when he left for office in the morning. I got some more angles from her that I am exploring now. Will call you as soon as anything relevant comes up,' it read. Ronit showed the message to Noor before returning the phone to his pocket. They were at the café entrance now and the scene that greeted them wasn't encouraging to the least.

The tiny space, with about half a dozen tables and a stand-up bar counter, was brimming with humanity. The tables were obviously all occupied, and there were people standing near the counter and in any empty space that they could find. Some had drinks in their hands, while others swayed hypnotically to the music. Social distancing norms were being flouted mercilessly and nobody seemed to care. The crowd inside the café, if it could be called that, mostly comprised young revellers of East European, African and Middle Eastern origins. Ronit was already feeling out of place, and he wondered how Sunil Bhatia would have managed to gel in with the crowd. 'Perhaps the place remains more inclusive prior to sundown,' he said to himself.

'What do you want to do?' he bent and screamed into Noor's ears to make himself heard over the pulsating music.

They were halfway through the sitting area, and she had paused twice to scan the surroundings already. Zhiming and Bhatia were nowhere to be seen, and it seemed highly unlikely that they were going to succeed in picking up their scent here. The only thing that Ronit could smell in the air was the heady, intoxicating odour of marijuana. If their target had left behind any clues, they were probably being trampled upon by dancing feet right now, and if someone had seen them, they were probably too inebriated to share their observations. Not to mention the blaring music, which made it impossible to converse even with a perfectly sane person.

'Follow me,' Noor mouthed, unmindful of his discomfort with the surroundings.

She led them to the bar, and bending into the barman's ears, placed their order. It was only when the tapster placed their drinks on the wooden counter that Ronit discovered what he would be drinking that evening. He was glad that it was going to be a pint of beer. He didn't particularly favour misadventures like drunken driving.

They stood there, sipping their drinks and watching the half-clad men and women making merry in a show of utter disdain for the supposedly agonising Delhi winters. Noor, by the purposeful look on her face, was still focused on her objective, but Ronit seemed as lost as a nun on a honeymoon.

He stood there listlessly as Noor tried to engage the busy barman in conversation. Forty-five minutes on, he was still sipping his first pint. Noor, on the other hand was on her third one and she had managed a few brief dialogue exchanges with the bartender too. Consequently, the man, Ronit noticed, was showering much more attention upon her. He had even placed a complimentary bowl of peanuts across her unless Noor had herself ordered it while she was whispering in his ears. And he seriously doubted that peanuts occupied so much mind space of hers that she would ask for them.

It was Noor who drew Ronit's attention towards the luminescence permeating through the fabric of his trousers. His phone was ringing inside his pocket. The noisy surroundings and the absence of vibrating alert feature in the phone model had nearly made him miss the call, but Noor was more alert than he had presumed. He drew the phone out, turned the screen for her to see the flashing number and inched his way out of the café.

By the time he stepped out in the alley, the ringing had stopped. Ronit called back, and after the second ring he heard Adhiraj's voice on the line.

'Bhatia's phone was switched on briefly. I couldn't get a precise location, but he seems to be somewhere in Paharganj right now,' he said. By now Noor had followed him out, and she was standing alongside Ronit watching his expressions change with every word he heard.

'He is saying that Bhatia is still in Paharganj,' he summarised for Noor's benefit, before shifting the call to speaker. 'Go on,' he directed Adhiraj.

'There's another thing… I was able to figure out how the girl established contact with Bhatia. It was through the dating app, Tinder. When I offered my help to locate him, his wife was quite forthcoming. I quizzed her about possible vices that could lead him into any kind of trouble, and she reluctantly admitted that he was a letch and would often ogle at women even when they were out together. He thought she didn't know that he chatted with girls on online apps, but she was aware of it and chose to play dumb. Like many typical housewives, she feared confronting him. She thinks that he was out with a girl a couple of nights ago, and he was in bad shape when he returned home the next afternoon. This latest dalliance might be behind his strange conduct and sudden disappearance, she feels.'

Ronit and Noor had reached their parked car by now. They sat inside and remained listening to Adhiraj. 'Tinder being the most popular dating app, I accessed the list of recently active accounts on their server. Through Bhatia's mobile number, I was able to find his profile. On his list of matches, I found the girl from the photographs too. It was on Tinder chat that they had arranged their meeting in Gurugram. It was their first meeting. She got him using a simple honeytrap it seems… Anyways, thanks to her profile on Tinder, I now have the number that she had been accessing the app from.'

'That's fantastic… Were you able to figure out where that phone is?' Noor jumped into the conversation.

'It's alright, she is with me,' Ronit had to clarify when the unfamiliar voice made Adhiraj go silent abruptly.

'Yes, that phone is switched on and is somewhere in Paharganj too. If we believe that both phones are at the same place, we can superimpose the earlier hit on Bhatia's phone with the new phone's location. The intersection of the two plots will give us a smaller perimeter to work with for identifying their precise location.'

'And how big an area will that be?'

'We will know exactly once I do the plotting, but my guess would be a distance of about a few hundred square meters.'

'That's still a lot for a congested area like this. Isn't there some way for us to pinpoint their exact location based on the phone numbers?' Noor persisted.

'There is actually,' Ronit chipped in. 'But for that we will have to track the GPS coordinates of her phone. The trace that Adhiraj has run so far is through the network owned mobile towers. It uses the signals received by these towers from a particular number to track it. In this case, the user doesn't know that the phone's movement is being monitored. However, with GPS tracking the software will send a signal directly to the instrument for detecting its location. Zhiming is bound to figure out that we are on her trail and are trying to figure out her whereabouts.'

He paused for the information to be absorbed, before explaining further, 'plus, it might require the device being used for the search to be in the vicinity and on the move. Adhiraj will have to come here with his laptop to carry out the pursuit.'

'Let me explain,' he added in response to Noor's puzzled look. 'GPS tracking is something like Google Maps, only it doesn't have a map to guide you in the background. So, you can figure out the coordinates of the phone from a distance, but to actually get to it you will need to have the device which tells you whether you are closing in on your target or moving away from it. It's not very different from the sort of trackers you see in movies or video games.'

'If we are ready to undertake GPS tracking, I can come to Paharganj right away,' Adhiraj added.

'Obviously, it's not the most favourable option, but we might have to consider it as a last resort,' Noor replied pensively. 'We don't have much time, and if nothing works, we might be left with no option but to reveal our hand… If we decide to go ahead, would you be able to come down here early in the morning?' she checked with Adhiraj. He was fully committed to the cause and confirmed that he would set out as soon as he received a signal from them.

After disconnecting the call, Ronit set the car in

motion and steered it in the general direction of their hideout.

Noor, after a brief contemplation, said to him, 'I think we will have to use the GPS route to find her... The fact that she has detained Sunil Bhatia for the night could only mean that she intends to strike tomorrow. She will probably accompany him to the Reserve Bank of India (RBI) office in the morning and use his login credentials to upload the malware on to the RTGS platform.'

'The Reserve Bank building is a high security zone. They don't allow visitors to go anywhere near the employee work areas,' Ronit countered.

'Maybe she intends to get Bhatia to do the upload, and she is accompanying him only to make sure that he doesn't develop cold feet at the last minute. If what she has on him is making him dance to all her tunes, there's no reason why it wouldn't force him to do this for her as well.'

'Or she might not be heading to RBI at all,' Ronit answered his own question, rolling up his eyes as if trying to read the subtitles of a suddenly occurring thought.

'RTGS is a widely used platform and a set of designated employees in every bank have restricted access to the network. They can simply walk into any bank branch, plug into the network and use Bhatia's credentials to sneak the virus in. No bank will turn down a request from a senior RBI official to let him work from their premises for a short while.'

'That's a logical point, and it might come in handy if she succeeds in giving us the slip in Paharganj. But the best place for us to catch her will be wherever she is stationed for the night. Out in the open, it will become almost impossible to apprehend her with the limited manpower we have at our disposal. She can duck out of view anywhere, and even if I call in some of my field agents, we will not be able to cast a dense enough net to prevent her escape. We must get to her before she moves out of her crash pad,' Noor responded.

'Why wait till the morning then? I mean, we are here already and Adhiraj said that he can join us... Why waste these crucial few hours?' Ronit asked impatiently.

'No, unlike popular perception, it is ill-advised to launch any clandestine operations in the early hours of the night. People are still alert then, and the chance that any unusual activity will be spotted and reported by someone is at its highest. Moreover, the cops would be vigilant against any suspicious movement too, especially in an area like that, and we don't want them to stop us for questioning, do we?'

Ronit hummed a response and let her carry on. 'In the wee hours of the morning the on-duty cops will be lethargic due to lack of sleep, while Zhiming's tribe will be disoriented as they emerge from it. The onlookers, if there happen to be any, won't have any reasons to look twice at a car plying on the streets either. That will be the most opportune time for us to swoop down on Zhiming.'

He accepted the explanation with a slight nod and kept his eyes affixed on the road ahead.

They drove in silence for a while, both dealing with

thoughts springing up within their own heads. It was when they crossed the IIT flyover that Ronit broke the prevailing silence. He had traversed these roads in his younger years, and he could say with relative certainty that they wouldn't encounter any checkpoints or police barricades enroute their destination now. This consciousness had infused a sense of relief in him, and his mind felt able to wander into other frontiers.

'You know, I still don't know what is it that you need from Zhiming so desperately… This is obviously not about establishing trust between us anymore, I trust you more than I have trusted anyone in a very long time, but I just can't seem to keep my curiosity at bay. Any chance that you can tell me about it now?' he said.

Noor turned to look at him and smiled. 'A promise is a promise, Ronit. I gave you my word that I will tell you all about it, and I intend to keep it. But can you at least hold on till we reach the safehouse? You need to be refreshed when you get up tomorrow, which means that you will need to catch some shuteye despite all odds. This could serve as a good bedtime story to put you to sleep,' she said in a tone that made him go weak in the knees. The next morning was going to be vital for them, but suddenly he felt more anxious about the hours leading up to it.

Chapter 20

Fish In The Net

New Delhi, 7-8 January 2021

Sunil Bhatia felt like a mechanical being, not having the ability to reason or think for himself. He had seen the pictures, and he knew that his life would turn into a living hell if they were to ever appear in public.

He was left with just one real option—to do what it took to keep them buried. So, he had resigned to the situation and to the diktats of the mystery woman, Sonam. He would go as far as he could, and if he were to fail still, he would put an end to his wretched life. Bhatia had arrived at this decision riding on a wave of intense self-loathing, guilt and desolation.

He arrived at the café five minutes before the designated time. He had planned to reach there by 5.45, but the place hadn't been easy to find. He stepped inside and walked up to one of the two empty tables. He couldn't see his host around, and he wasn't disappointed. In fact, just the thought of facing her again was making his belly churn.

The Soul Café wasn't the sort of establishment that Bhatia would ever visit on his own. It was a small place, almost dingy, with graffiti laden walls. While the bar counter was made of solid teakwood, other furnishings in the rectangular space were a random mix of garden, patio and lounge furniture pieces. An assortment of tables, chairs and stools picked up from scrap dealers and yard sales perhaps—an artful collection of distressed furniture. The place had about seventy percent occupancy at even the odd hour, and most patrons appeared languid and sluggish as though they had been there for a while. The feel of the place wasn't lively and vivacious as the name might suggest, instead it exuded a laidback and meretricious vibe.

She appeared in the doorway at precisely six, paused to look for him and stepped forward. The scene reminded Bhatia of their first meeting from a few evenings back. His heart was pacing just as rapidly as it had then, only for an altogether different reason now.

'Hi, nice to see you again,' she said, smiling as she parked herself on the empty chair. She was behaving as if she had already forgotten all that had transpired when they were together last.

'Hi,' Bhatia returned, finding his voice with much effort. 'Why have you called me here? What do you want from me?'

'Don't worry about that. Have something first,'

she returned nonchalantly, waving to catch the server's attention. Without bothering to check with him, she ordered a beer pint for him, the same brand he had been drinking on their first date, and a sweet lime soda for herself.

'Tell me, what is it that you want?' he asked again, in a near whisper once the waiter was gone.

'You just can't stop worrying, can you? Fine, I will tell you what I want… I want you to take me somewhere with you. It's that simple. Does that settle your curiosity?'

'Take you where? And what do the pictures have anything to do with it?' he shot back.

'Oh, those pictures! They are worthless, really. I intend to destroy them as soon as you do this one simple thing for me,' she responded nonchalantly. 'And while I would have loved to tell you more about where you will accompany me and why, unfortunately I am not in a position to do so. But if you keep doing what you are told, this whole thing will soon be behind you. Trust me.'

'Trust you?' Bhatia said scoffingly.

Sonam's words were laden with hope, but they seemed too good to be true. All she had asked was for him to take her someplace; she hadn't posed any impossible demands and she hadn't asked him for money either. That is what made it utterly unbelievable for Bhatia, unless there was more to her demands, and she was deliberately keeping the full picture concealed from him.

'Your scepticism is understandable, but you will see in the end that I was right,' she said with a sense of reassuring inevitability.

'So, let's get it done and over with then. Let's go, I will come with you.'

'We will, but first switch off your phone and give it to me. And yes, finish your beer,' she said, pointing to the untouched pint. Bhatia did as he was told, gulping down the contents of the bottle in one go. Sonam checked his phone to ascertain that it was off before depositing it in the back pocket of her denim. 'Don't worry, this is only for safekeeping. You will get it back in the same state as it is now.'

She left a 500-rupee note on the table and led him out of the café. She was walking briskly and Bhatia, with his bulk, was struggling to keep pace with her. She led him out of the alley to where his car was parked, and positioning herself beside the passenger door, said, 'Let's go.'

It was weird that she knew exactly where Bhatia had parked his car, but Bhatia was immune to being surprised by anything that she did. Sonam had stretched the boundaries of his belief to a point where he had stopped measuring her actions on the scales of probability and possibility. He silently unlocked the vehicle and slipped inside.

Bhatia steered the vehicle through the winding streets of Paharganj until she asked him to stop and park on the roadside. He did as he was told, and as he was stepping out of the vehicle, his eyes caught the glow sign board hanging outside the building which seemed to be their destination. 'Hotel Delight,' the board read. Bhatia froze instantly, his shoulders stiffening and eyes widening in trepidation. The horrific memories of the time when he had last entered a hotel room with Sonam descended on him like a stinging swarm of bees.

'Don't worry, you are not walking into another photoshoot. I already have what I want, and another set of photographs will not be of any use to me whatsoever... This is just a stopover before we head to our destination. Just follow me and you will be alright,' she said, gauging his predicament.

Bhatia knew that she was right. Sonam had no reason to subject him to the same trauma all over again. The pictures she had in her possession were enough to make him come to heel. And yet, the dread of finding himself alone with her in a confined space was proving difficult for Bhatia to shake away. He followed her in measured steps, looking pale and stricken.

As they stepped inside, they were greeted by the sharp smell of burning incense. Up ahead was the lobby, adorned by a single sofa set upholstered in dark maroon velvet. It might have been decorous in its prime, but big round patches were visible around the cushion and back pillows now. A centre table with a pot stuffed with plastic flowers sat across it. To the left was a wooden counter, and a boy in his mid-twenties was seated behind it, bearing a bored look on his face. He spared them a brief glance as they turned away from him, towards the staircase. The receptionist's reaction, or the lack of it, told Bhatia that the girl's face wasn't unfamiliar for him—she was probably renting out a room in the hotel already.

She led them up two floors to a landing which had passages branching out on either side. Bhatia had to pause to catch his breath. The climb had him panting as if he had just completed a full marathon. She turned right and waited at the mouth of the passageway for him to catch up. They crossed four numbered doors, two on each wall, and walked up to the one straight ahead of them—Room Number 203. Using a keycard, Sonam opened the door and let them in.

It had the musty smell typical of dingy rooms in low-budget hotels. The interiors were typical too, not strikingly different from the room in the Gurugram hotel.

'Sit down,' she said, offering Bhatia the lone chair. She sat down on the bed herself, facing him.

'Why are we here?' Bhatia asked her circumspectly. As much as he tried, he was unable to make sense of things. He couldn't come up with any probable reasons to explain their presence in the room. And the ensuing uncertainly was only working to compound his fears.

'Like I said, we will head out to our destination from here…,' she said, adding, 'tomorrow morning.'

'What? I can't spend the night here,' Bhatia shot out. His forehead was creased with tension, and it seemed as if he would burst out crying any minute. 'Let me go… I will meet you in the morning and take you wherever you want to go. But please let me go right now,' he pleaded.

'I would have done that if I could, but I can't. You are here for the night, that's a given. Now, whether you want to spend your time crying, or you want to relax and think about tomorrow when this will all be behind you, is entirely your choice,' Sonam replied.

The jovial tone in her voice had given way to a more authoritative one, and Bhatia could tell that she meant business. He was going to spend the night in that room, no matter what. The optimist in him made him repeat the request a couple of times, but he had to give up eventually.

'Now that I have nowhere to go, can you at least tell me where we are going tomorrow?' he said, intending to extract what he could from the conversation.

'Yes, that I can tell you now,' she said, taking him by a bit of surprise. He hadn't really expected her to yield so simply. 'We will be going to the HFD Bank in Connaught Place. You will introduce yourself and ask the manager to let you work from the bank premises for a couple of hours. All I want is a few minutes alone with your laptop when it is connected to the RTGS network. You could take a quick trip to the restroom perhaps, and I will be gone by the time you return,' she said.

'What do you want to access the network for? What are you planning to do?' he returned, with a faint quiver in his voice.

He knew that she couldn't siphon off funds using his login credentials; that would involve multilayer approvals, and even if she did initiate such a transfer, there was no chance for it to go through unchecked. However, using his security clearances, she could get into the heart of the system. He couldn't think anything that such an ingress might serve for her, but he was certain that whatever she was planning wasn't something simple or benign.

'Oh, there are some transactions that I need to validate. That's all,' she said. And then, as if reading the signs of concern on his face, she added, 'Look, I agree that what I intend to do isn't entirely legal, and if it gets out in the open it could land you in trouble. But the fact is that there is no way that my actions can be traced back to your system. Therefore, you are at no risk unless you volunteer to tell them about it yourself.'

Bhatia wanted to believe her, but a voice in his head was warning him against doing so. After all, she was the same woman who had lured him into a room and stripped him of all his pride and dignity not very long ago.

'You may choose not to believe me,' she said, reading his thoughts precisely, 'and I owe you no explanations either. I could have simply told you what I want you to do, and I suspect that you would have followed even if the task happened to be way more hazardous. The only reason I am telling you all this is because I empathise with you. I understand the agony that you have endured and the helplessness you feel, and it is not something that I am particularly proud of. But now, when you are one step shy of making all your problems disappear, I want you to truly believe that you have overcome the worst. I want you to approach tomorrow without any hesitations or uncertainty.'

As she was speaking, Sonam stepped behind the chair and planted her palm on his shoulder. Her words were compassionate, as though they were coming straight from her heart.

'You know, by accompanying you to the bank, I will be exposing myself too. The CCTV cameras will capture us entering the premises and there will be witnesses who would have seen us together. Now, if there was any chance of the leak being connected back to you, why would I put myself at risk? I would have simply asked you to go there on your own and get the information out. I am only doing this because I know that they can't link this to you unless you decide to open your mouth.'

'You are not exposing yourself. With the photographs in your possession, you know that you can force me into taking the entire blame,' Bhatia returned warily.

'Yes, I do have the photographs, but do you think they will actually protect me if the authorities were to identify you as the source of the leak? You have never been questioned by the cops, have you?' Bhatia didn't offer a response. 'You will be singing like a canary even before they actually lay a hand on you. Trust me.'

'And then, you will tell them how the photographs were forcibly clicked and used to blackmail you. They will give assurances that they will apprehend me and stop the photographs from being revealed, and you will take the bait and offer them your full cooperation. For now, you might think that the situation could play out any differently, but it will not. So, you see, the photographs won't remain much of a shield for me then. The only way that I can stay undetected is by keeping you insulated, which I will be doing,' Sonam reassured him.

Bhatia believed her because he wanted to, and because

there was nothing else that he could really do. He could only pray that the girl knew what she was talking about, and that the technology experts at RBI would fail to identify his login as the source of the breach.

He took a few minutes to collect his thoughts before he spoke again.

'But I can't just land up at any bank branch unannounced. We have a system in place for that. I will have to inform my boss and send an advance email request to HFD Bank.'

Sonam considered his words and asked him to go ahead and do what was needed. Bhatia messaged his Boss informing him of his absence from office. The reason he gave was that he needed to visit a bank branch for reviewing their RTGS processes. There was nothing unusual about this, as Bhatia was expected to undertake such field visits as a part of his job.

Next, he typed an email to HFD Bank's liaison officer, informing her that he will be visiting their Connaught Place branch the next morning. Sonam had been peeking over his shoulder the whole time, and as soon as the email message was sent, she repossessed his phone and switched it off once again.

They ordered their dinner in the room, and shortly after they were done eating, Sonam offered him the bed to retire on.

Bhatia was too spent to bother about courtesies or even consider if his companion deserved any. He accepted the offer and slumped down on the bed instantaneously.

When he finally shut his eyes, Sonam was still in the room, occupying the chair and staring fixedly into the screen of her laptop.

Chapter 21

The Backstory

New Delhi, 8th January 2021

Ronit was the first to excuse himself and recede to the bedroom.

Noor had been oscillating between her laptop and phone, deliberating with her superiors and channelling the resources at her disposal to ascertain that they were prepared for every conceivable eventuality. In a few hours, their operation would be underway. They would be pitted against a ruthless and astute adversary, against whom even a minor slip was likely to prove fatal.

Noor's thoroughness was warranted and even oddly comforting for Ronit. Unable to make sense of the things she was doing or the language she was speaking, he had decided to leave her to her own devices and get some rest instead.

It had seemed like a great idea, especially when his tired bones sank into the soft mattress at once. But the respite was only momentary. The restlessness he had been trying to contain was soon out in full bloom and he found himself twisting and turning uneasily on the bed. It was only when he heard the shuffling noises of Noor winding up her wares that he was able to put a stop to it.

'You haven't slept yet?' she asked, slipping beside him on the bed.

'I am trying,' was all he could murmur.

Ronit and Noor had been together for the entire day, and yet there was something about this moment that was making him lose his voice. He felt like a wax statue being approached by a flow of smouldering lava.

She pulled herself towards him, and placing her hand on his head, said, 'And now, about the promised bedtime story.' Ronit's eyes shut involuntarily as he felt her fingers meander across his scalp.

'My name is indeed Noor,' she began, 'and I am from Malaysia. Unlike India, in my country the balance of power between the military and the civilian government is tilted in favour of the former. The military top brass has traditionally been involved in all vital political decisions concerning our country. Our Generals have always wielded considerable power and it is believed that their blessings are essential for any party to form a government... This background is essential for you to comprehend the importance of what I am about to tell you.'

Ronit had forgotten all about the assurance that she would tell him the reason behind her pursuit of Zhiming. With Noor's advent to the bedroom, he had lost his awareness momentarily, but her words had done well to veer him back to reality. He was attentively listening to them now.

'One of our earlier Generals, a revered man credited for ushering Malaysia into the new era, had three wives. The last one was a European diplomat he had met at the peak of his power. It was a whirlwind romance. Within a few months of their first meeting, she moved to KL, and they got married. The wedding was widely covered by the world media. However, the very strength that draws two strong-willed individuals towards each other can sometimes become a bane for their harmonious coexistence.'

Barkha's face flashed before Ronit's eyes at Noor's description of the General's marital life. Their situation wasn't very different than the General's, he pondered, before pivoting his attention back to the story.

'The wife was quick to realise this and also the fact that the General's ego wouldn't allow her to walk away from him even if she wanted to. She knew him well enough to grasp that while she could try to lead a comfortable life in the shadows of his immense might, she must also do what she could to protect herself if the situation were to worsen. She was a diplomat, and so she was not only sharper than his other wives but was also capable of identifying consequential pieces of information that she chanced upon while in his proximity. She started saving these pieces—maps of military and nuclear installations, confidential order copies and agreements on covert actions that each government takes to protect itself—as a bargaining chip to help her preserve her life and freedom if the eventuality arose.'

'Their initial years together went by in a breeze, but then the cracks in their marriage began to show. The frequency of their public appearances started to wane, and if rumours are to be believed, they quarrelled like cats and dogs behind the porous walls of their bungalow. Over the years, she had collected enough evidence to bring down not only her husband but his entire country. She had fortified herself with information that made her untouchable. So, a few years back, she packed her bags and returned to Switzerland.'

'Of course, she was expecting the General to react, and so she had taken all the accumulated proof along with her. This is where she went wrong with her judgment. The general never retaliated. He was a tough man to get along with, but he had loved her with all his heart. He accepted her decision without a protest and left her to her own devices, until she was diagnosed with a life-threatening illness. When he became aware of it, he left no stone unturned to provide her with the best medical care possible. He flew in doctors and equipment from across the globe, and he prayed for her recovery. The only thing he never did was pay her a visit. This was one thing that his vanity didn't allow him to do.'

Noor might as well have been narrating the script of a potboiler to him. There was drama, there was suspense and there appeared to be an impending climax. Ronit was fully absorbed.

'By the time she could muster enough courage to own up to her mistake, it was too late. She could only manage to send him an email before she breathed her last. It was an expression of remorse and apology from a dying woman to the only man who had ever truly loved her. It was obviously touching. But the email also carried a detailed account of the documents she had sneaked out of Malaysia. She sent him the details of the bank locker where she had stored them and the authorisation code that would grant him access to it. The email melted something within the General and he called her, for the first time since she had gone away, but the phone went unanswered. This was shortly before the news of her demise reached him.'

'But where is the link to Zhiming in all this?' Ronit asked, unable to contain his curiosity.

'Patience, my friend, patience.' she said, smiling. 'The General did what he needed to do next. He sent a team of agents to extract the incriminating documents from the locker and destroy them. It was a small team, as the task assigned was simple and no hurdles were expected along the way. But an unanticipated twist awaited them at the bank. They were informed that the authorisation code had been changed and they could only access the locker with the help of the new code. You know how stubborn the Swiss can get on such matters. Despite requests being routed through the highest levels on both sides, the bank remained uncooperative and refused to grant them access.'

'You mean, the General's wife had lied to him in

her email?' 'No, she had not! Somebody had hacked her email and digitally altered the authorisation code in the bank's records. What the lady didn't know was that her relationship with the General had made her an obvious target for multiple intelligence establishments. She had been on their radar ever since she set foot in Switzerland.

We had our suspicions about which one of these agencies might have orchestrated the hack, but that wasn't going to lead us anywhere. We couldn't start chasing anyone based on conjecture alone, so we set up a tight vigil in and around the bank. Whoever was in possession of the authorisation code had to visit the bank to claim the contents of the locker. That was our only chance to plug this potentially devastating leak.'

'Let me guess,' Ronit said, 'it was Zhiming who turned up to access the locker.'

'Yes, but it wasn't quite as simple as that. The documents held in the locker are so explosive that they could turn Malaysia into a pariah for the global community. We couldn't let them get in the wrong hands at any cost. For several months we had our agents keep round the clock watch on the bank, we were compelled to turn modest bankers into informants—in some cases, by using tactics that might not sit well with your conscience—and we had to set up a team to intercept and analyse every single piece of correspondence that the bank or its employees engaged in. This was by far the most intensive covert operation that I have ever witnessed, but it did lead us to Zhiming in the end.'

'If you found Zhiming, why didn't you apprehend her? I mean, with such an elaborate set-up in place, how could she give your people the slip?'

'Zhiming had come to Switzerland knowing fully well that we would be watching the bank. She assessed our fortifications from a distance and decided that trying to access the locker wasn't worth it. She suspended her plans to extract the documents and left the country. All we could manage in the end were two pictures that were captured by a CCTV camera in the vicinity of the bank. Which, by the way, was a remarkable feat, considering that none of the renowned global agencies even knew what Zhiming looked like till then,' Noor said, making a case for what her outfit had managed to achieve.

'So, she doesn't have the documents with her then?' Ronit enquired.

'No, she doesn't, not yet at least. But the trouble is that the Chinese don't need the documents to be in their possession to make us dance to their tunes. The General's wife had inventoried them in her email, and so they know exactly what the locker contains. The fact that they are in a position to retrieve its contents is sufficient for them to hold our government to ransom. We are in no position to defy them until the documents are well beyond their reach. This was perhaps the reason why they didn't rush to claim them as soon as the authorisation code had been changed, or why Zhiming was willing to defer her plans to recover them. Having the authorisation code gives them the same leverage that possession of the documents would.'

'You want the locker's authorisation code from Zhiming then?' Ronit surmised.

'Clever, Mr Biswas, clever indeed,' she returned with a smile. 'It appears that my company is starting to show some effect after all,' she said, placing her head on his outstretched arm. Ronit turned and planted a gentle kiss on her forehead. Noor shut her eyes and her smile widened ever so slightly.

'You have a busy morning ahead… If I were you, I would try and get some sleep now,' she said, after a moment of quiet.

Ronit shut his eyes once again, but his mind was far from resting. Much later, when his thoughts finally dissolved into the silence of sleep, he was still grappling to comprehend the nature of his feelings for Noor.

What transpired between them the previous night could be attributed to their carnal longings, but not what he was experiencing today. Her petite frame ensconced beside him on the bed was making him feel complete and alive once again, despite the threat and uncertainties looming in the distance. The longing he felt today was more visceral and more real, and it seemed to intensify with every minute he got to spend with her.

At that moment, Ronit would have gladly given a hand and a leg to know what was going on in her mind.

He knew that she cared for him too. He could say so based on her words and her actions. But there was no way for him to tell how innate this care of hers was. Was it just a cocktail of compassion, guilt and companionship, or was it something deeper and more enduring? Or, like him, was she also struggling to put a finger to the thread that was binding them together?

Chapter 22

Taking The Plunge

New Delhi, 8th January 2021

Ronit had been asleep for just over three hours when, against the combined resistance of his corporeal senses, he was aroused by what he thought was a massive quake. For the first bleary seconds he tried to make sense of his surroundings, almost ready to take cover if the roof were to come crashing down. It didn't. Then, sensing a human presence in his proximity, he turned to find Noor standing by the bedside.

'Finally,' she said, pulling back her hands which were already positioned to give him another shake.

'Oh, hi,' he said, struggling to pull himself up. 'What time is it?' he added, rubbing his eyes with the back of his hands.

'It's almost quarter past four. I have been trying to wake you up for over ten minutes now,' she grumbled.

Her words brought about a sudden realisation of the

onerous task facing them, and Ronit was out of the bed in a flash. Noor looked ready and raring to go already. He was struck by a sharp stab of guilt. Wondering whether she had managed any sleep at all, he went about readying himself hurriedly.

By four-thirty, the two had stepped out of the house and were making for the parked car. Noor was clad in khakis and a denim jacket, with a black tank top peeking from underneath it. The jacket sleeves were carelessly folded, and she carried a small backpack, making her look like an unruly college student.

She walked purposefully to the car, used the remote to unlock it and slipped inside on the passenger side. When Ronit got in on the driver's seat, she was waiting with the ignition keys dangling between her fingers. 'I know, I am guilty of pulling you out of bed, but you might want to consider dropping that grumpy look of yours. It doesn't suit you one bit,' she said playfully.

Ronit couldn't help but smile back at her. Noor had this uncanny ability to make light of the most strenuous situations, making him feel safe and confident in her company. It had taken her all of two sentences to relieve him of the weighty burden that had made the brief walk to the car seem like an uphill climb.

'Best of luck, Noor,' he said softly. 'To you too, Ronit,' she responded, returning his smile.

The city was yet to emerge from its slumber, making their drive smooth and brisk. In precisely twenty minutes they were at the Connaught Place outer circle, closing in on the bus stop where they had agreed to meet Adhiraj.

The lighting—a muddle of the natural grey-blue of an onsetting winter morning, and the shades of white and yellow originating from manmade sources—was still inadequate. So, when Ronit noticed two human silhouettes waiting under the shelter instead of the one he was expecting, he was somewhat alarmed. He approached them cautiously without compromising the speed of the vehicle. Only, when he was close enough to identify them did he bring the car to a screeching halt. Sitting beside Adhiraj, looking eager but composed, was Myra.

'Why did you ask her to come?' Ronit said concernedly in response to their greeting. He was addressing Adhiraj, as he got inside the vehicle and settled behind Noor. Myra had already occupied the rear seat on his side by then.

'Sir, do you really think that I would be here only if he asked me to?' Myra was the one to respond.

Ronit wasn't able to see her expressions, so he couldn't determine the exact connotation behind her question. It could have been anything from a show of affection to an expression of disappointment over his presumptiveness. He let it pass. Myra was already inside the car, and she was heading to Paharganj with them whether he liked it or not. He couldn't just drop her anywhere at this hour. The decision had been made and no amount of fretting on Ronit's part was going to alter it now.

'Do you have everything you need to track the phone's location?' Noor, coming to Ronit's rescue, asked Adhiraj.

Adhiraj was already pulling his laptop out of its case

by then. 'Yes, I just need to connect this to the hotspot, and I will be ready. I have also plotted the area where they are likely to be found based on the information from the mobile towers. I think we should take a quick round of the area and identify pockets where the probability of their presence is higher—sections with greater concentration of lodges, hotels and other rent-a-room establishments. It will be better if I switch on the GPS tracker as close to their location as possible. They will have that much lesser time to react once the tracker pings their phone,' he said.

The logic was spot on and was greeted with consenting nods from other occupants of the vehicle. Adhiraj had been entrusted with the task of leading them to their target and they were happy to follow his lead. Ronit, relying on Adhiraj's directions, was soon turning the vehicle inside Paharganj.

'The area to our right,' Adhiraj said, bending slightly to look out the window on Myra's side. 'If the two phone instruments are at the same place, they will be somewhere here. We will drive around the highlighted zone in the map and when we are back here, we can decide where to begin our search,' he said, meaning to alert the others.

Paharganj is a multifaceted locality catering to diverse human needs. Small shops selling everything from trinkets to hippie clothing, eateries serving global fare at rock-bottom prices and a slew of budget guesthouses make it a haven for international backpackers. It is around the needs of these customers that the pulsating nightlife and neon-drenched avatar of Paharganj has evolved.

Its proximity to the New Delhi Railway Station and the availability of economical stay options means that it receives a constant traffic of domestic travellers and night cappers who dribble out of the station gates in hordes, only to be absorbed by Paharganj's winding alleys. There are clusters of *Vaishnava Dhabas* (roadside eateries catering mainly to pure vegetarian Hindus) and pure vegetarian restaurants catering to the appetite of this set of customers, affordability being the major factor distinguishing them from their more glamorous cousins in the area.

And then there are the locals—families who have been living in the area for generations. They thoughtlessly dump their garbage on the roadsides and park their vehicles haphazardly, and their children play cricket in the alleys, just like the residents of several other parts of Delhi. Together they—the residents, domestic travellers and international tourists—make sure that the lanes of Paharganj never sleep. The pandemic had eerily quietened these bustling lanes, but Paharganj appeared to be getting back on its feet already.

Even at the early hour, Ronit could see human activity all around him—walking tourists tugging their heavy bags with them, ragpickers doing their morning rounds with grimy gunnysacks dangling over their shoulders, sputtering autorickshaws with customers peering out to find hotels that they had made reservations with, and eateries being readied to greet their first customers of the day. There was little that separated one street from the other, and Zhiming could be holed up just about anywhere, barring perhaps the small residential cluster they had just crossed.

'Everyone, keep looking ahead and act normal,' Noor said all of a sudden. 'Keep driving, don't slow down and take the next right turn,' she said to Ronit from the corner of her mouth.

Her eyes were affixed on the road and her face was expressionless. Anyone who happened to glance at Noor from the outside would only see a girl indifferent to the tedium of being driven to her destination early in the morning.

The others were startled by her abrupt eruption, but they were quick to gather their bearings and follow her instructions.

'Park the car wherever you can,' she said moments after they had taken the turn.

'What happened?' Ronit asked, easing the vehicle behind a parked tempo traveller.

'You didn't see him, the guy sitting on the bench at the tea stall we crossed? It was the same man who was behind Zhiming at the Metro station—a part of her security detail,' Noor explained.

'Are you certain it was him?'

Noor didn't bother to answer in words. She looked back at Ronit in a manner that made him cringe. He would have withdrawn his question that very instant if he could.

'We are as close to our target as we can get. She is in one of the buildings lining the street we just crossed.

Do you want to start the GPS tracker now?' she said to Adhiraj.

Before Adhiraj could respond, Myra jumped into the conversation. 'There was just one hotel in that lane—Hotel Delight—and it was right across the road from the tea stall. I didn't see any other lodging options nearby. If she is somewhere there, she must be in that hotel,' she said.

'It's certainly worth a try,' Noor said after a momentary pause. 'Anyways, the GPS tracker can at best point us to the building where she is. We will still need to figure out her precise location on our own. We should check the hotel first. If she is there, we will have the advantage of catching her off guard. And if we don't find her, the choice will be between using the GPS tracker and capturing the Chinese man and getting him to spill the beans somehow,' she said to no one in particular. It was as if she was crystalising the next course of action in her words rather than in her mind.

'But with that guy keeping watch, how are we going to get inside the hotel undetected?' Ronit asked once Noor was done talking.

'Myra and I could distract him,' Adhiraj offered.

'That could be dangerous. He is a trained operative and neither of you have any field experience...'

'How do you intend to create the diversion?' Noor asked, interrupting Ronit midsentence.

Adhiraj offered his half-baked thought, and they spent the next few minutes in discussing and refining it.

Expectedly, Noor was doing most of the talking. Ronit refrained from further voicing his concerns about sending Myra and Adhiraj in harm's way. This was partly because he had realised the need to deploy all resources available to them and partly on account of his growing confidence in Adhiraj's idea.

'It is clear then—you will drive out of here and park the car in the next lane. If our target is in the hotel, we will give you a missed call. That will be your cue to call in the backup troops. Get them to detain the guy outside and wait for our call before entering the premises. If you don't hear from us within thirty minutes of the missed call, give the men a go ahead anyways. We would need you to rescue us then… And if she is not in the hotel, we will meet you at the car directly,' Noor said, summarising the last leg of the detailed plan she had just laid out.

Adhiraj, following her instructions, had called the Paharganj police station and shared his RAD credentials with the station incharge, requesting him to keep a police team on standby. He had explained that his colleagues and he were investigating a lead in the area and there was a possibility that their targets might put up some resistance. Using persuasive terms like national security and highly confidential operation, Adhiraj was able to successfully deflect the curious questions that followed his request. The call concluded with the PSI assuring him that a team of ten armed policemen would be waiting to start out on his command.

Ronit had offered to make the call since all

departmental coordination with external agencies had been routed through his office at RAD, but Noor politely refused. 'Let Adhiraj place the call. After all, he will be their liaison once you and I are inside the hotel. Moreover, we don't know if the CBI has looped in the police department in their search for you. If they have, then your call will have them mustering their men alright, but in pursuit of an entirely different target,' she reasoned.

Noor had placed a call of her own while Adhiraj was busy impressing his ask upon the station incharge. She shot out a set of brief instructions before disconnecting. 'My operatives—I have a couple of them deputed on the ground here. I was telling them to remain alert as we move inside the hotel. I don't intend for them to partake in the action, but if the situation were to take an unexpected turn, they might come in handy,' she explained to Ronit.

Ronit understood the underlying complications of unauthorised involvement of foreign operatives in a tactical on-ground operation, and he conveyed it to her with a nod of his head.

Once Adhiraj and Myra had confirmed their understanding of precisely what they were expected to do, Noor reached inside her backpack and extracted a Webley & Scott .38 calibre revolver. Extending it towards Ronit, she said, 'It is loaded. I hope you won't need to use it, but just in case.'

Ronit took the weapon with tentative hands and slipped it between his belt and the small of his back. He knew how to use the gun alright, but he was yet to fire a shot at anything that moved and breathed. He certainly wasn't looking to change that today.

Next, Noor pulled out some other objects—a small sachet, plastic luggage locks, a pair of handkerchiefs and similar inconsequential items—and relegated them to the pockets of her khakis. The last thing she pulled out was a menacing Glock 44 pistol and slipped it into her waistband. In the brief duration that the weapon had remained in her hand, it looked big and dangerous for her petite frame, like a child ready to ride a motorbike. But the resolve in her eyes was telling. Ronit could sense that she was more than willing to pull the trigger if she needed to. The thought sent a frosty shiver down his spine, only exacerbated by the cold metal he could feel rubbing against his skin.

Having satisfactorily concluded the transfers, Noor swung the backpack over her shoulders and stepped out of the car. The other three followed suit. Ronit, after locking the vehicle, handed over the keys to Adhiraj and the four of them started walking casually. They were walking away from the car, in the direction opposite to where they had come from. It was time to set Adhiraj's plan into motion.

Chapter 23

The Charge

New Delhi, 8th January 2021

Adhiraj and Myra reached the mouth of the lane in which Hotel Delight was located. They were about a dozen steps ahead of Noor and Ronit.

A circuitous walk had brought them to the same place from where their car had turned inside the lane some time back. The hotel, with its pale green façade, was roughly a hundred steps ahead, to the right side of the street. Across it was a roadside tea kiosk, its walls a collage of brightly-coloured posters, with two wooden benches placed on its sides. One of them was occupied by their target, a seemingly bored man tinkering with his phone to weather the monotony of his assigned task. As far as Adhiraj could see, other than him and perhaps the teaseller ensconced inside the kiosk, there was no one else around. This augured well for what he planned to do next.

He turned around to catch Noor's eye for a fraction before staggering inside the lane. On cue, Ronit and Noor slipped behind a parked autorickshaw—a vantage point that allowed them to keep an eye on the street without the risk of being seen themselves.

Adhiraj was walking with the sway of an inebriated man leaning and tugging on Myra who was holding him by the arm. It wasn't an unusual sight for these parts. A lore among addicts was that you could procure any kind of hallucinogen on the streets of Paharganj if you knew where to look. Wasted men and women, boys and girls, after a night of frolicking and substance abuse at one of the many underground clubs, were often found sprawled on the streets the next morning, and the lucky ones could be seen being dragged away by their relatively sober companions. Adhiraj and Myra were playing their parts to perfection.

The tea stall was still a few metres away when Adhiraj took a misstep, bumped into Myra, and reflexively bounced away from her in an exaggerated compensatory attempt. The momentum made him lose the little control he had on his body, his steps faltered, and he fell down with an unmistakable thud. Ronit winced at the sight, biting his lips to stop a shriek from slipping out. He could tell that Adhiraj had taken an actual fall to make the enactment seem real.

Myra screamed though, as she rushed to help Adhiraj. At first, she tried to lift him on her own, struggling to even move his slumped frame. She looked left and right desperately, and that was when she caught the eyes of the man who had been carefully observing everything. 'Help,' she screamed out to him.

The man continued to stare back at her blankly, as though unsure of what he should be doing. 'Please help me, he is badly hurt,' Myra pleaded. He gave the street a fleeting gaze, perhaps hoping to spot a willing volunteer to take his place, and finding no one, he slowly got up from the bench.

Myra remained pleading hysterically while he covered the little ground that separated them. 'Please help. He is bleeding. He needs a doctor. Our car is parked just around the corner, please help me take him to it.' Adhiraj remained unresponsive, his eyes shut and head resting in her lap. He was convulsing frighteningly every now and then.

The Chinese man bent down to place Adhiraj's arm around his shoulder, and then, in an astonishing display of strength, he jerked him to his feet in one swift motion. 'This way,' Myra said, getting up to support Adhiraj from the other side. The man followed her direction without voicing a word.

Noor and Ronit watched them walk away, an insentient Adhiraj propped between the two frames, his head bobbling with each step they took.

'They've done well,' Noor whispered, 'it's our turn now.'

As the trio approached the turn, Noor stepped out in the open and made for the hotel in brisk steps. Ronit was right behind her, breathing deep to assuage his rapidly beating heart.

They didn't have much time. The lookout had left his post reluctantly and he was sure to return as expeditiously as he could. They, on the other hand, were faced with the tough ask of disappearing inside the building without calling undue attention upon themselves. The tea stall owner would notice any unwarranted urgency in their behaviour, and if he were to relay his observations to the man, their game would be over even before it began.

Ronit let out a relieved sigh once they were safely inside the building. Meanwhile, Noor was confidently striding across the lobby and making for the reception counter. She tapped her knuckles against the wood, making a sleepy head rise behind the desk. The young receptionist looked back at them, first grudgingly— not happy with the disturbance—and then with a spark of curiosity. His eyes went up and down, like the readings on an ECG graph, scanning Noor and Ronit from top to bottom, lingering a little longer as he soaked in Noor's frame.

Ronit was expecting her to recoil in embarrassment or burst out irately, but she wasn't done surprising him yet. 'We need a room,' she said brusquely, her mannerisms akin to those generally associated with girls working the streets.

'For how many hours?' the boy asked. Ronit placed his origin to in some part of Eastern Uttar Pradesh or Bihar on the basis of his accent.

'Two hours,' Noor returned. 'How much?'

'One thousand… advance,' he said.

He was probably expecting her to negotiate, but when she placed a pair of crisp 500-rupee banknotes on the counter, a glint appeared in his eyes. Pocketing the money swiftly, he emerged from behind the counter and asked them to follow him. The warmth of the currency notes had successfully negated the need for the obligatory entries in the guest register and even the mandatory identity checks that the law of the land expected him to undertake.

He led them to a room on the first floor and pulled out a keycard from his pocket. 'This is our best room… the honeymoon suite. And this place is totally safe. If you decide to come here more often, I could even extend a special discount for you,' he said solicitously to Noor, as he swiped the card in the slot. Noor smiled at him noncommittedly, eagerly waiting for the door to open.

The receptionist had only taken his first step inside the room when Noor slammed the door behind them, grabbed him by the scruff of the neck, and propelled him forward. She shoved him on the bed with the same disdain that she would dump an unsavoury half-eaten sandwich into the wastebin.

It had all happened in a flash, leaving him with no time to even register a protest. By the time he could turn on his back to face her, the nozzle of Noor's pistol was already tracing a circle in the small space between his eyes.

'What is your name?' she asked, the words somehow

slipping past her gritting teeth.

'Ravi... Ravi Kumar,' he stammered, trying to look at her without disturbing the piece of metal that separated them.

'Ravi Kumar... Do you want to stay alive?' Noor continued, pushing the gun against his head.

Ronit could see that she was furious, perhaps peeved at the humiliation she had been subject to by the ignorant receptionist.

'He seems like a sensible man. Why don't you let me have a word with him, I am sure he will be happy to cooperate with us,' Ronit said, stepping forward and gently placing his palm on her outstretched hand. Noor hesitated for a second, and then she stepped back, leaving the floor to Ronit.

'Ravi, we are officers from RAD. You know what RAD is, don't you?' Ronit said cordially. Ravi nodded his head vigorously, droplets of tears finally escaping his eyes to run down his cheeks.

'Good! So, you would also know that this little scheme you guys are running in the hotel is of no interest to us. It is usually the bigger fish that we go after, not the small fries. We are here because we want some information about a gang of criminals that we are chasing. If you answer our questions truthfully, nothing will happen to you. In fact, you might even become a hero if your information proves helpful in leading us to them. But if you choose not to help, or decide to misguide us, we will be forced to haul you to Tihar jail right away. You will come out of jail eventually, in five or maybe seven years, but your life will never be the same again. So, choose wisely, Ravi. What is it that you want to do?'

'I will do whatever you tell me to do, Sir. I won't lie to you, I promise. But please don't take me to jail… please don't…,' he pleaded with folded hands. His face was contorted strangely, as if he could start wailing any minute.

'Do you recognise them?' Ronit asked, shoving the images of Zhiming and her bodyguard in Ravi's face.

A flicker of recognition emerged as soon as he saw the pictures.

'Yes Sir, they are staying here at the hotel, Both of them,' he said animatedly.

The fear had suddenly vanished from his visage, and he now looked excited and eager to assist them. It seemed as if the photographs had given him not only hope but also a purpose.

'They came here two days ago, these two and another Chinese man,' he started, without waiting for Ronit to pose his next question. 'They have taken two rooms—one for the girl and one for the two men—but who knows who sleeps in which room at night. But last night the girl was in her room, I know, and she had a customer with her too. I myself served them their dinner in the room. The men, they keep coming in and going out every few hours, even through the night. So, I can't say for sure if they are in their room right now.'

'Which room numbers? And how many other rooms

in the hotel are occupied right now?' Noor stepped forward and asked.

'Room numbers 203 and 206, Madam, on the floor above this one. The girl and her customer are in 203. Those are the only two rooms occupied on that floor and there is an elderly couple on this floor, in Room 104. They came last night and have a train to catch later today. Because of corona, we are not getting many customers, Madam, that is why we are forced to let out rooms by the hour. Otherwise, Hotel Delight is a very decent place, you can ask anyone,' he replied.

Ravi answered their remaining questions with equal fervour, not giving them any reasons to doubt his sincerity. He even handed over his mobile phone and master keycard willingly to Noor when she asked for them. It was when Noor asked him to lie down on the bed and pulled out the luggage locks that he looked a tad disappointed.

'This is for your own safety,' she explained, 'to keep you away from anything that happens while we try to bust them. We will come and get you once it is all over. And yes, we will also ask the Paharganj police to issue a letter of commendation to you.' By the time Noor stepped away from Ravi, his hands were bound behind his back and his feet bundled together, and yet the purposeful glow on his face was back.

Before they left the room, Noor tugged at the wire that linked the phone instrument in the room to its socket and stepped on the plastic connector. It disintegrated with a crunch. Ronit used this time to dial Adhiraj's number, disconnecting the call after three rings. With Ravi confirming Zhiming's presence in the hotel, they were one step away from accomplishing their mission and it was vital for all the meandering pieces of the plan to come together now.

'206 first,' Noor whispered, after spending a few seconds to study the layout of the floor.

Noor then extracted a bottle from her backpack and a handkerchief from her pocket. She soaked the inner fold of the fabric with droplets of liquid from the bottle before returning both items to their original places. 'Let's go,' she whispered again.

Ronit noticed Noor extracting the master keycard and her gun as she tiptoed forward. He pulled out his own weapon and held it in his hand, walking close on her heels. She stopped at the door and placed her ear against the wood.

Ronit couldn't tell if she heard anything but, in a few seconds, she pulled back and signalled him to follow her. She swiped the keycard gently and pushed the door to create a small fissure. Ronit watched in awe, scared to even let out a breath, as after a brief pause Noor tiptoed inside the room. The pistol in her hand was trained and ready to cough lead out of its belly at the slightest tremble of her finger.

Noor moved very slowly, minutely observing every sight and sound for any warning signs, until the bed and the human form lying on it came into her view. She glanced at Ronit, returned the pistol to the safety of her waistband and pulled out the handkerchief from her pocket. She crept to the bedside and pressed the fabric hard against the nose and mouth of her oblivious target. The man suddenly opened his eyes, but Noor was ready for him. She was using her left hand to choke him, leaving her right hand free to handle his resistance.

As soon as his eyes opened, she pressed his right hand with her knee and landed her elbow on his chest. The man winced in pain, his scream muffled by Noor's hand, and he swung his free hand wildly at her. By then she had flung herself over him and was sitting on his chest, her left hand affixed on his face like an iron claw. She intercepted the blow and slipped his hand under her other knee. The man continued to resist, wriggling, twisting and trying to use his feet to push her away, but to no avail. He was pinned to the bed and there was no way for him to free himself from Noor's clutches.

Soon the tension in his limbs completely disappeared, indicating that the brief resistance was over. Noor climbed down, leaving his slumped body on the bed, and looked at Ronit who was glaring at her with horror-stricken eyes.

'Don't worry, he's not dead,' she said. 'He'll regain consciousness in an hour or so.'

The Chinese agent's comatose state did not stop Noor from exercising all the precautionary measures that she had deployed while securing Ravi in the earlier room. Only, this time, instead of making a clean exit, she made a brief stop to uproot the jet spray from the attached bathroom. As they stepped out of the room, she stuck the faucet between the door handle and frame in such a manner that it made it impossible for anyone on the inside to open the door. It was an improvisation to serve as an external lock for the hotel door which wasn't exactly designed to detain people inside.

'Now to the final frontier,' she whispered to Ronit, who was still reeling under the shock of watching her subdue the Chinese operative with her bare hands. They made their way to the door in soft, measured steps, and Noor once again put her ear to the door. This time though, she remained listening for a relatively longer duration, her expressions changing as rapidly as London weather. Finally, she waved Ronit behind her, prompting him to take cover.

Placing her thumb on the peephole, she knocked thrice on the door. A faint bustle followed, and then they heard the faint click of the lock being disengaged. Slowly, the door parted. Noor had slipped slightly to her left, keeping herself concealed from view, forcing the occupant to expand the opening. Moments later, they saw Zhiming's unmistakable profile appear in the crack.

In a sudden, sharp move, Noor landed the butt of her pistol on Zhiming's face and kicked the door with all her might. Zhiming staggered back and fell, giving Noor the opening to barge in and pounce on her. Ronit rushed inside behind Noor.

The Chinese agent was on the floor with blood oozing from her nostrils, and yet she had the alertness to flip sideways and greet Noor's approaching frame with a powerful mid-air kick. The impact was such that it changed the trajectory of her jump, sending her crashing against the wall. She lost her grip on the pistol and it went flying down to the floor.

Ronit instinctively reached out to secure the weapon first, only to find another pistol lying not far from it on the floor. The second gun, he surmised, must belong to Zhiming, and Noor's unexpected assault was probably responsible for its separation from her. He claimed both the weapons, and just as he was securing them in his pocket, his attention was drawn by a sudden movement on the bed.

The commotion had awakened Sunil Bhatia, who was now pulling himself against the backrest, eyeing the happenings with incredulity and disbelief. To him it was like exiting one nightmare only to slip into another one.

'Stay where you are, Sunil Bhatia. You move a muscle and I will shoot,' Ronit warned, his words belligerent and dripping with viciousness. Bhatia had witnessed enough troubles over the past few days to dissuade him from even entertaining the idea of defying a gun-wielding man.

'I won't move… I won't move,' he said frantically, pulling his knees close to his chest and bundling himself in one corner of the bed.

Meanwhile, the women wrestled it out on the floor. Ronit could see that Noor had found a more than able match in Zhiming. The fluidity and speed with which the Chinese was moving made Noor seem like a pugilist battling it out in a higher weight category.

Suddenly Zhiming used a leg grip to flip Noor on her stomach. She planted her knee on Noor's spine and, grabbing her by the hair, jerked her head upwards. Noor let out a guttural scream, which seemed to pierce through Ronit's innards. Gripped by sudden rage, he stepped forward and hit Zhiming on the head with the butt of his revolver. The weapon was heavy and he had swung hard. She held her head between her hands and slipped down from her position of advantage.

Noor, without wasting a blink, positioned herself behind her and wrapped her arm around Zhiming's neck. Using the pressure of her arm to assert control, she guided Zhiming to the chair and made her sit down. 'Cover her and don't hesitate to shoot if you have to,' she said, urging Ronit to point the revolver at Zhiming's face.

She took out her trusted plastic zip ties and bound Zhiming's wrists and ankles to the chair. Noor then deposited a burst of slaps across her face. It was her victory dance, her response to the hardships she had endured for the past many months on Zhiming's account, and had Ronit not intervened, the thrashing might have continued well beyond her last breath. Such was the fury welled up within Noor.

'Bitch,' she said in utter disgust, reluctantly pulling away from her. Ronit remained covering Zhiming with his gun, unable to trust the little strings to keep her contained.

Noor returned soon, and standing next to Ronit, she said, 'thank you.' Though the fatigue of the fistfight was still visible on her face, she had done well to regain her composure quickly. Ronit glanced at her and smiled.

'You know, I have been dreaming about this day for a long time. And now that it is finally here, it is hard to believe that this is all going to end today. I am already dreading the void that it will leave behind in my life. Strange, isn't it?' Noor said. She held a glass vial in her hand, and as she spoke, she was transferring its contents into a syringe.

'What is this?' Ronit, upon espying her actions, asked warily.

'Oh, this is Sodium Pentothal—an advancement of science that will save me the trouble of pulling her nails out with a plier. It is also referred to as truth serum by some. In a few minutes I will have what I need, and she will be all yours as promised,' Noor replied, stepping forward to administer the injection.

Zhiming shut her eyes as the plunger emptied the liquid in her bloodstream. Noor waited for a couple of minutes before tapping her cheeks to bring her back to life. She responded with a slight shake of her head and opened her eyes slowly, only now they seemed narrow and disoriented. Her eyebrows were pulled together and there was a confused look to her. Noor peered into her eyes, and satisfied with what she saw, she asked Zhiming, 'What is your name?'

'Mei Yang,' she said with trembling lips.

'Do you work with the Ministry of State Security in China?'

Zhiming looked back at her in bewilderment. She then surveyed the other faces in the room, none that she seemed able to place, before returning an affirmative nod.

'Here,' Noor said, pushing a small pad and a pencil towards her. 'Write down the new authorisation code for the Malaysian bank locker in Switzerland. You remember the locker, right?'

Mei nodded, reaching out for the paper and pencil. She stared blankly at the paper for a few anxious moments before half-heartedly scribbling something on it. Noor almost snatched the paper from her hands once she was done writing. She glanced at it, her lips curving into a smile as she did so, before surrendering it inside her pocket. Her job was now done. She had lived up to the expectations of an entire desperate nation and the exhilaration she felt was no less than that of a climber scaling the peak of Mount Everest or an Olympian having delivered a gold medal-worthy performance.

'It's time for you to call Adhiraj,' she said to Ronit. Turning towards Bhatia, she added as an afterthought, 'and maybe we should let him get out of here first.'

Ronit nodded. 'Come on, get up and get out of here. A police team will be here soon, and if you don't want to be dragged further into this mess, make sure that they don't see you anywhere near this place. And if you ever talk about anything you witnessed here today, you will be opening yourself to an investigation that is bound to outlast your remaining years. You understand that. Don't you?' he said to the man. Bhatia, though still holding his original position, looked a lot less frightened now.

'Yes, Sir,' he said. 'But before I leave, can I ask her one small question too?'

'Where are my pictures?' he asked Mei upon receiving Ronit's nod.

She studied his face for a few seconds before pointing a lethargic finger towards the area under the window where her laptop case was propped against the wall. Bhatia stepped forward and extracted the brown envelope containing the prints that had pushed him into a miserable and petrifying realm.

'And the soft copies?'

'I don't store such gory things on my phone,' she said, cocking her head and looking at Bhatia from the corner of her eyes. She looked like a spoilt brat sulkily justifying her actions when being reprimanded for them. 'I had deleted them as soon as we got the prints.'

'Thank you,' Bhatia said to her instinctively. 'Thank you… Thank you,' he added, spinning around to look at Ronit and then Noor. The relief he felt was overbearing, and he was clearly struggling to express it. 'I will go now… Thank you,' he said, turning towards the door.

'Wait,' Noor interrupted him. 'Don't take the front exit, that would be under surveillance. Look for another way out or hide somewhere within the hotel building until the cops leave,' she suggested.

'Thank you,' he said once again, nodding his head in acknowledgement, before exiting the room.

'I will get going too,' she said, watching Ronit pull

out his phone.

As their eyes locked, she stepped forward and planted her lips on his. Ronit wrapped his arms around her and shut his eyes. The kiss was brief, but it carried a much deeper meaning than what words could ever convey.

'I hope that we meet again, perhaps in a glossier chapter of our lives,' she said, stepping away from him and turning towards the door. Ronit watched her receding form, until she turned in the stairway and could no longer be seen.

Letting out a deep sigh, he called Adhiraj. Twenty-six minutes had passed since he had last dialled the same number.

It would be a few minutes before the police team got to the room, and he decided to put this time to good use.

There were questions that were troubling him, questions that the girl bound to the chair had answers to, and she was as willing to answer them as she would ever be. Recognising his only chance, he stepped forward and crouched down in front of the chair.

Chapter 24

The Day After

New Delhi, 9th January 2021

Ronit was relaxing on the couch, holding the teacup between his fingers. The abandoned laptop screen flickered on the centre table, doing what it could to catch his attention. Ronit had been scanning the news headlines when Barkha materialised with another cup of tea, his second since waking up, making him divert his attention.

This was an unusual scene for the given hour inside the Biswas household. Generally, Barkha and Ronit would be well ensconced in the clamour of a new day much before the clock struck 11 am. But today was an aberration. Ronit had taken a much-needed day off from work and he seemed in no mood to let habit-induced urgencies come in the way of his unwinding.

The past couple of days had not only drained him physically, but they had also convinced him to reconsider his priorities and pursuits of life in general. He hadn't got the time to further engage in this existential deliberation yet, but he had made a resolution. Ronit was henceforth going to approach life at his own tranquil pace rather than trying to match its unsettling rapidity. This was an attempt by him to underline his individuality, a refusal to let the bigotry and uncertainties he had experienced at uncomfortably close quarters define his identity. Hereafter, he was going to do the things that truly made him happy.

The awakening wasn't alien to him either. Ronit had experienced it while holding his dying father's hand in the dank hospital room, and he had felt it as he helplessly watched the pandemic butchered humanity all around him. It was a sensation he was familiar with. It lasted for days, sometimes weeks, until life and its prescribed ways succeeded in seducing him all over again. For now, though, his passions were on a rise and he appeared committed to his pledge.

It had all started when, after Zhiming's arrest, Ronit returned to RAD with Myra and Adhiraj. Most of the faces he encountered on the way to his department were indifferent and oblivious, cocooned from reality by their own blissful ignorance. He encountered faces looking at him with cautious curiosity—those who had been fed varying bits of information about him through the office grapevine—trying to decipher the climax to the yarn in their heads by scrutinising his countenance. He could see the relief on them—of getting a ringside view of a full-contact combat sport instead of having to partake in the bout.

There were a few who seemed genuinely concerned too. Yadav, for instance, materialised in his cabin minutes after Ronit had stepped inside himself.

The senior official was pleased to see him, and when he asked a simple two-worded question, 'What happened?,' Ronit knew that he couldn't escape the one thing he had been dreading the most. It took him a good fifteen minutes to summarise the happenings for Yadav's benefit and an equal amount of time to field his questions. Through the glass partition, he could see that Myra and Adhiraj's situation was no different. They were both surrounded by colleagues, cornered into conducting storytelling sessions of their own.

Shortly after Yadav left, he received a call from the Home Secretary, Mr Gupta. It was no surprise that Gupta was aware of the broad contours of what had transpired—after all, the National Investigation Agency (NIA), the agency that had obtained Zhiming's custody from Delhi Police, was under his direct administrative command—but he wanted to hear the details from the horse's mouth. Ronit obliged, responding temperately to the heaps of praise that Gupta showered him with. He didn't display much enthusiasm even when Gupta promised to propose Ronit's name for a prestigious gallantry award. The award, given Ronit's state of mind, was nothing more than a symbol of the meaninglessness he was itching to get away from.

The call lasted for about twenty minutes, but sadly it wasn't the last of Ronit's ordeals for the day. He had to file a formal report to the CBI, a prerequisite for the agency to close the investigations that had been initiated against him, forcing him once again to reminisce the happenings with considerable minuteness.

He successfully circumvented curious enquiries garbed behind solicitude and counsel, but not every single one of them. There were colleagues he was friendly with and those he felt obligated to provide straight answers to, making it impossible for him to deflect them all. After two more narrations, Ronit decided that he had had enough. He glanced at his watch—4.00 pm—before striding out of the cabin and down the lift. He wasn't carrying an office bag and that only made his escape smoother.

He called Barkha from the taxi to inform her that he was heading home. He had last spoken to her on his way out of the Paharganj Police Station. 'The ordeal is finally over,' he had announced to her. She had heaved a sigh of relief and gradually the lustre of her voice had returned. She was disappointed to hear that he would be heading to office first, but when he explained she understood the need for him to apprise his superiors and file a report on the matter. 'Come soon, I will be waiting,' she had replied.

Barkha had indeed been waiting for him, for she opened the door as soon as he stepped on the landing. She paused to look at him, before springing forward suddenly. She held him in a tight embrace, as if fearing that he might disappear again, with tears streaming down her eyes. 'I got so scared,' she finally spoke with a quiver.

'Let's go inside,' Ronit responded, gently stroking her hair.

Ronit narrated his ordeal to her, this time of his own accord, leaving out sections warranting exercise of confidentiality, over tea and biscuits. Barkha remained listening, dove-eyed and dismayed, neither interjecting nor posing any questions. She seemed glad just to be sitting beside him and listening to his voice. Ronit did not bring up the details of what had transpired between Noor and him. It was a deliberate omission, of course.

Noor had been a mirage, a passing hurricane that had left him uprooted from within. He would think about her, he would feel the touch of her skin against his and he would play scenes of their communion in his head over and over again, but that would be his chastisement. His and his alone. He couldn't share his pain, his longing, with anyone. Not even Barkha.

Noor was gone and he wasn't sure if he would ever see her again. She had reminded him how love felt, and she had made him feel alive again. The memories he had made in the brief time that they were together would last him a lifetime. They will always remain in his heart—the euphoria of a treasured past and the anguishing knowledge that he would never relive those moments again—tugging and pulling at him. And like a true masochist, he would keep returning, seeking comfort in their benign indulgence.

'You look tired,' Barkha observed, suggesting that he retire early and offering to serve dinner whenever he was ready for it. She had prepared *Bharta* and *Kheer*, his favourites.

By 7 pm, they had retired to the bedroom. Ronit could feel the exhaustion of the adventure deep inside him, with unknown bones and unfamiliar tendons twinging and throbbing at random. He had expected sleep to consume him immediately, but his mind had other plans. It posed a question, setting his thoughts on an unexpected course. 'What would Mei Yang alias Zhiming be doing?', it asked.

Zhiming was probably at one of the NIA's undisclosed detention facilities, being worked upon by the best in the business. By the time they were done with her, she would have revealed everything from her favourite ice-cream flavour to the specifics of her sinister plan to paralyse the Indian economy.

Noor's assessment had been accurate. Zhiming's scheme was indeed to sabotage the RTGS network and bring the already ailing economy to a stuttering halt.

In the little time he had with Zhiming before the police stormed into the hotel room, Ronit had learnt that the Chinese had set their plan into motion long before he was first approached by Noor. The military confrontations on the borders, abetting and manipulating the agitating farmers and the well-orchestrated Maoist attacks in the hinterlands were all distractions meant to keep the Indian security apparatus on its toes. The added stress that these acts put on the government coffers and the corresponding political tumult were only further embellishments.

Ronit tried to ascertain whether the coronavirus had

been unleashed on the world by the Chinese, as was being alleged by certain sections of the media, but he didn't get a conclusive response. If indeed the virus had been deliberately deployed, Mei Yang was not involved in the operation.

Mei had been entrusted with the most crucial leg of the Chinese operations in India—to pave the path for unobstructed flow of their investments into the country. This, she intended to achieve by turning India into a pariah for global investors. Her first target was to weaken investor confidence in the Indian stock markets by highlighting their volatility and flawed fundamentals to the world.

She named four listed entities whose share prices she had sent tumbling down with a little nudge, one of them being C K Ramanathan's organisation. This case had come under spotlight only on account of Ramanathan's suicide. Else, Zhiming's handiwork was almost impossible to detect. The RTGS network was meant to be her final blow, and she was well on course to deliver it until Noor and Ronit showed up on the scene.

Ronit was vaguely familiar with the NIA's interrogation processes. Truth serum or not, in a few days they would have traced every bit of information from Mei's brain into their systems. That was when they would break the news of her capture. Her masters in China would of course be aware of the developments already, but they would be required to make a formal statement only after the disclosure by the NIA.

Going by China's track record, they were unlikely to accept anything. They would probably insinuate that Mei Yang was just a tourist and India had wrongfully detained her. They would shout and scream in international forums, while more rational negotiations would continue in parallel behind closed doors. Her masters would know that a captured spy was as worthless as a used napkin, and they would not be willing to yield much to secure her freedom.

Finally, in a few years when the matter would have slipped out of public memory, the Chinese would make some minor concessions and India would release her in return. This was the standard path that all such cases traversed, and there was no reason why Zhiming's case would turn out any different. As far as Ronit could tell, for the foreseeable future, Zhiming was going to remain a reluctant guest of the Indian establishment.

Ronit didn't know when his consciousness detached itself from Zhiming's thoughts and he was able to fall asleep, but when he woke up, Barkha was standing on the bedside holding a tray with two cups of tea. The digital clock on the nightstand was displaying 9:07.

He remained in bed for another hour, soaking in the relative peace and quiet of a new day before the need to visit the washroom made him emerge from it. Instead of returning to the bed, he made for the living room and slumped down on the sofa.

He opened his laptop and began skimming through the main news stories of the day. Ronit wasn't expecting any of the news agencies to have caught wind of Zhiming's arrest, but his curiosity wouldn't let him rely only on the plausible. He had to ascertain it for himself.

The majority of the news items he came across were centred around the Covid-19 vaccination drive, which was set to commence in a week. He read about a soldier of the People's Liberation Army (PLA, the Chinese Army) who had transgressed across the LAC near the Pangong Tso lake and had been taken into custody by Indian troops deployed in the area. He was yet to come across any mention of the arrest of a Chinese citizen from the Paharganj area of Delhi by the time Barkha materialised with a second cup of tea.

They sipped their tea quietly, staring at the nothingness surrounding them and glancing at each other intermittently. Ronit noticed that Barkha looked different this morning. She had the same tentative demeanour that had first made him fall in love with her, and in her eyes, he saw a longing and an appreciation that he had not seen in a long time.

'It's late… I will get the breakfast ready,' she said, picking up the two empty cups and heading for the kitchen. Ronit watched her disappear into her war zone before reaching out for the laptop once again.

He was about to click on the browser when an unfamiliar icon on his desktop caught his attention. He moved the cursor over it curiously until he could read the name of the application in the pop-up. It was a restricted software used for cloning communication devices belonging to suspects who were under investigation. This wasn't a legitimate ploy and discoveries made via this route were not admissible in court, but jurisprudence had hardly ever defined the methods used by covert functionaries. It was the end-purpose that mattered to them, as it had when Ronit had used the software to clone Barkha's phone.

He let the cursor linger around the icon, fully aware that with a simple click of the mouse he would have an unfettered insider's view of Barkha's life. He would know exactly who all she had been talking to, when and for how long, in the time that he had been away.

He would know who Anmol was and what was brewing between Barkha and him. He was tempted to click the mouse instantly, but he waited for the initial surge of curiosity to settle. He clicked on the icon and gradually scrolled down the options visible on the pop-up window.

He paused on *Open* momentarily, before continuing further down. When the pointer reached *Delete*, he paused again and clicked on it. As he watched the heavy file being deleted from his system, a strange calm seemed to descend on Ronit's visage. It was the calm of a man ready to reclaim the reins of his life.

Acknowledgements

It is usually the author's name that graces the cover of a book. Sometimes, this appears to be a trifle unfair, as there are many who contribute behind the scenes to make a writer's idea, a reality.

"Thank God, it is over.... You will be able to spend more time with me now," my daughter said to me when I was finally done writing this manuscript. Her words sum up the sacrifices made by the family and friends of a storyteller.

I am eternally grateful to my wife, Neeru and my daughter, Naisha, for standing by my side in this journey. Always!

A big thank you to Suhail of The Book Bakers, a friend and an amazing publishing agent whose contributions to Indian publishing will be spoken of, many years hence. Thank you, also to my editor, Abhijit, and the amazing team at Vitasta (Saumya in particular), who have made this journey a seamless and memorable one.

Of course, the culmination of it all is what you are now holding in your hands. Thanks for choosing to read *Operation Bamboo Garden*. I hope it meets your expectations. If you have any feedback or comments to share, please reach out to me on Instagram or Facebook (@authoranuraganand)

About the Author

Anurag Anand, an acclaimed writer, is also an award-winning artist, corporate professional and devout family man. He is a familiar face at literary events across the country. His columns appear regularly in publications like *ET HR World*, *The Times of India*, *Suburb Live Magazine* and *Readers Choice*—a global ezine. *Operation Bamboo Garden* is Anurag's fifteenth book.